Maybe
may appeal m
does for me gu

Love

Chris

CW00953417

Little Shar

by

Chris Corbett

ISBN: 978-1-291-22244-9

PublishNation, London

www.publishnation.co.uk

DEDICATION

To my dear mother.

ACKNOWLEDGEMENTS

To Marilyn Joice and all at the Northern Branch of the Jane Austen Society and also to Lucy Adlington of 'History Wardrobe'.

Many thanks.

Chris Corbett.

LUCY ON THE SCREEN

As with Jane Austen's major characters, interpretations of Lucy have varied considerably in nature. The BBC serialisation of 'Sense and Sensibility' shown in 1981 (with Irene Richard as Elinor Dashwood and Tracey Childs as her younger sister Marianne), saw Julia Chambers' Lucy Steele at her most ingratiating and fawning. By contrast, in the best known adaptation of the novel, the 1995 film where Emma Thompson starred as Elinor and Kate Winslet was Marianne, Imogen Stubbs played Lucy as a femme fatale par excellence. The most recent adaptation (2008, again a BBC production (Hattie Morahan as Elinor and Charity Wakefield as Marianne)), gave a different slant again with Anna Madeley's blend of sugar sweet craftiness. Proof if proof were needed in all these excellent performances of how, for some of us, Jane Austen's most compellingly modern, pragmatic and successful of heroine foils may be viewed!

INTRODUCTORY NOTE

One of the confusions often existing with 'Sense and Sensibility' (and for that matter 'Pride and Prejudice' also) is that, while the as it were 'original drafts' for these novels were written by Jane Austen in the 1790's they were not actually published until considerably later (1811 in the case of the former). In their quiz book 'So You Think You Know Jane Austen' (Oxford University Press 2005), John Sutherland and Deirdre le Faye do mention however certain pointers to indicate the setting is in the former period (for example Marianne Dashwood's hairstyle and the needlebooks given to Lucy and her sister Anne by the mean Fanny Dashwood). It is thought that the author began work on what was first entitled 'Elinor and Marianne' around the year 1795. At this stage it may have been an epistolary work, but was in a third person or 'narrative' format probably at the latest by 1798 and this is the date that I have assumed for the events described in 'Sense and Sensibility' for us. Lucy Steele, when we first meet her there is described as 'not more than two or three and twenty'.Thus,in the year of Trafalgar, she is thirty.

Furthermore there are some minor points of language and custom to consider for the purist. One example for a modern readership is to refer to Mrs 'Lucy Ferrars' rather than Mrs 'Robert Ferrars'.Thus, whilst attempting to retain a flavour of the language and, still more so, the conversation of the day it is not a Regency manuscript. Nor is it in any sense an attempt to imitate Jane Austen's style. For me that would be the height of presumption. On the other hand I have genuinely attempted, so far as Lucy is concerned, to be as faithful as possible to her creator.No doubt those readers familiar with 'Sense and Sensibility' will recognise certain phrases and words used by Lucy Ferrars when she was Lucy Steele. This is quite deliberate.Unlike the other characters in the stories Lucy is not mine. She is only borrowed. Lucy Steele (as was), has a distinctive style of speech and her lapses in grammar when they occur demonstrate all too clearly her lack of 'literacy'. It must remain a very open ended question as to whether 'time and conscience', or social ambition and experience, obtained as Mrs Ferrars, would have eliminated such 'faults' .For the purpose of this story I have taken something of a middle path, believing that the desire and application have brought a wider vocabulary and command of her native tongue, but have still not removed all of those delicious phrases and inconsistencies created when her original character was so beautifully and expertly 'drew' for us!

'Thank you', cried Lucy warmly 'for breaking the ice; you have set my heart at ease by it; for I was somehow or other afraid I had offended you by what I told you that Monday.'

'Believe me' and Elinor spoke with the truest sincerity, 'nothing could be further from my intention than to give you such an idea. Could you have a motive for the trust that was not honourable and flattering to me?'

'And yet I do assure you', replied Lucy, her little sharp eyes full of meaning, 'there seemed to me to be a coldness and displeasure in your manner that made me quite uncomfortable.'

Jane Austen.

'Sense and Sensibility' (Chapter 24).

CHAPTER ONE

' RAT IN A BONNET'

It had been the most difficult case so far for Mrs Lucy Ferrars. Not that she had any doubts about the innocence of her client, but it seemed, that, with each question that was answered, a more demanding one took its place. Now, face to face again with the one who had escaped a conviction for murder and a hangman's noose, broad smiles replaced anxiety.

She turned away from the mirror. Certainly it was true that herself and Robert had never been the ideal couple. Yet to free herself from the shackles of a loveless marriage by killing a husband ? Ridiculous. Only three months before she had investigated a similar affair and Viscountess Cramlingbourne had not succeeded in avoiding the gallows. But Lucy's marital state had been far less unpleasant to bear than that of the young and headstrong Catherine Cramlingbourne. In six years herself and Robert had lived amicably apart, her own existence funded not only by by an ample allowance, but also by some fine investigative skills. The girl who had started out in life as poor relation Lucy Steele now moved, as Lucy Ferrars, amongst the highest in Bath's society.

The case against her had simply collapsed. For a time of course, as with anyone in such a situation, she had seen nothing beyond freedom, but now it was time to consider the puzzle. Robert had disappeared in Devon (where for some peculiar reason he had chosen to live amongst some of Lucy's nearest and very far from being dearest), while she was resident in Bath. Turning again towards the mirror with an air of self satisfaction that word 'innocence' came back to mind. She could not resist a sly ironic smile. Hardly a characteristic most, if any, would have associated with the name Miss Lucy Steele! Before her marriage she had made more than one enemy. Was this the place to start delving then? Mrs Fanny Dashwood had never truly forgiven her she was sure, for all the apparent harmony. Then there was Lady Middleton. Or even her own sister Anne? The smile now was replaced by a snort of contempt and a half laugh. Hardly Lucy. Hardly! Nancy had all the subtlety of a carthorse and the quiet introspection of a waterfall. 'Oh my dear Lady Middleton a thousand pardons for my interruption. I have put the poison in Mr Ferrars' wine as you instructed - oh I promised not to speak of that in company did I not?' Why, mused Lucy irritably, was I cursed with such a stupid plain sow of a sister?

What some might have considered to be the most capable of foes she completely dismissed. Any differences which did exist between herself and the woman who had married Robert's elder brother were not of relevance here. Elinor Ferrars, pondered Lucy, possessed both a keen mind and, unless time had been more severe upon her than usual since their last meeting, also considerable beauty. In short the only one in the whole family worthy of respect. But if she could keep secrets and, yes, plot and plan, nobility of character would prevent mischief. How anyone with such abilities could be content buried in the country amongst cattle was a mystery in itself. In her way Lucy considered Elinor to be almost as witless as Anne.

She had been, save for her maid Henrietta, alone at her rooms in Queen Square exactly half an hour. Now however an insistent knocking upon the door, followed in rapid succession by the briefest of conversations below and a hurried running up the stairs, ensured that thirty minutes of solitude would not become thirty one. The door flew open and Lucy just had time to rise from her seat before being hit by a lilac gowned and bonneted tornado.

'You are here! Oh Lucy. Dearest dearest Lucy. How very good it is to see you once more. I have been far from idle. But can you ever forgive me?

'I assure you there is nothing to forgive' replied Lucy Ferrars with a little smile. 'Rather the contrary for I understand that it is yourself whom I must thank for persuading Miss Bellingham and Lord Cottam to speak on my behalf. Without you I should not be at liberty. Come', she concluded, finally wriggling free of a tight embrace to look her companion in the face, 'is that not so?'

Miss Caroline Westbrooke took Lucy's hands in hers as she

responded to this query.

'Well yes. Of course. But that is not, quite, my meaning.'

'Indeed? Let us sit then and tell me why I should be vexed. Though I can think of nothing less likely.'

'How I have missed you. Did you not think the whole world against you?'

'I never doubted your loyalty Caroline. You and you alone I trust.'

'Thank you' replied Miss Westbrooke in a tone of voice Mrs Ferrars was a little surprised by. She put her head a little to one side and observed her companion.Their time apart had done nothing to dim Caroline's dazzling and quite exceptional beauty, enhanced still further by a passion for pretty clothes.Nor had those large soft green eyes lost any of the tenderness and sensitivity that they had always betrayed. But now there was something else amongst the perfect decorative confectionery. Not poise either, still less vain self assurance. Those too had always been present. No, to the mix that caused an envious admiration to women and which cast a constant spell of enchantment over men, was added a quiet and stern resolve.

'When I have discovered who has said those things', continued Caroline Westbrooke, 'they shall regret it. For I esteem no one, not even my father, higher than yourself.'

'We are certain made very different', responded Lucy with just the semblance of a smile, 'for you have always shown me much affection. However, what sensibilities I do possess are entirely yours. Your father forbade you to help me and yet you ignored his wishes. That weighs much with me. Those who might have helped you, I think chiefly of Rebecca Frobisher and Catherine de Traile, left Bath as soon as I was, er, 'removed'. Your aunt also desired you to return to Tinterton Manor I presume?'

'Yes. But I would not. So my father came to fetch me back himself. He said he had been brought proof of your guilt and, in Laura Place would you believe it Lucy, shouted up to my window. Ordered me, me his own daughter, to come down the stairs and into the carriage. I opened the window and shouted back telling him I would not and had locked my door. So he went away in a high temper. What do you think of that?'

3

'Since all know that Viscount Westbrooke is devoted to, as he said at Lord and Lady Norwells' when we visited there last spring, 'my beautiful and radiant princess', his actions, notwithstanding any suspicions of myself, do seem rather curious I agree. Did aught else occur after?'

'Yes there was something', replied Caroline, 'a gentleman very much desires to meet with me.'

Lucy raised her eyebrows. 'I should be amazed if all gentlemen did not want to do that! Have you filled up your book of suitors yet or merely opened a second one?'

Miss Westbrooke turned her head away to hide a contented, almost smug, smile.

'Oh I have never kept written records! But, no, it is not that this time. What I mean to say is that he, or rather of course a servant, brought two letters. This very morning. One for me, the other for yourself. I kept it here for you in my little box.'

Lucy proceeded to read the correspondence now handed to her.

Mrs Ferrars.

You have escaped and I rejoice at it. If you wish to do your country a great service and be well rewarded may I request that you meet with me tomorrow at eleven in the morning at Miss Westbrooke's rooms in Laura Place. I have requested the same from her as I know that lady to be of an excellent character and totally worthy of our trust. Speak to no one but herself, for the matter is a most delicate and secret one, so much so indeed that further communication would be most foolhardy. If, when I call, I am informed that you are not receiving visitors I shall take that as answer in itself to my request.

Lord Minto.

After a brief discussion the ladies' decision was that his journey would not be wasted.

'My congratulations upon your freedom Mrs Ferrars', Minto began to

Lucy and then, with a little bow to Caroline, 'Miss Westbrooke.'

'I thank you my lord', answered Lucy after the answering curtsies. 'I had not realised the extent of my, that is I should say, of Miss Westbrooke and myself's, reputation.'

Minto smiled. 'Indeed Mrs Ferrars. I know that you work best hand in hand. Viscount Westbrooke and I are old acquaintances.He values his title, but not so much as his horses, they not so much as his estate and that not a half of the pride he takes in his beautiful daughter. Her slightest wish is a firm command. But I am certain that she knows that already.'

'No indeed I do not Lord Minto' responded Caroline, moving to stand shoulder to shoulder with Lucy. 'There is now a distance between us. Moreover, if he believes that I require my inheritance he is greatly in error, for I have my own income from my work.Like yourself I am thankful that Mrs Ferrars is at liberty, but I fear that father does not share that sentiment.'

'I believe that he does Miss Westbrooke' , came the flat reply. Answered yet more flatly.

'I know his opinion of Mrs Ferrars my lord. You do not. Inform him when you see him next that he will have to tie me up to take me back to Tinterton and there is little purpose in that. For', added Caroline, taking Lucy's hand and giving her a tender smile, 'I shall only run back again.'

'Letters may be read Miss Westbrooke by other than the desired recipient of them. So your father could not state his true feelings to you. This way it will be thought, by any observer of his behaviour, that he disapproves of your friendship with Mrs Ferrars. Your affection for her is widely talked of.'

Caroline reddened and replied with considerable testiness.

'Mrs Ferrars is my best friend Lord Minto and I flatter myself that I am also hers', (here Lucy nodded). 'But if the implication is that our 'affection', as you see fit to call it, goes anything beyond..'

Minto put up his hand. 'It is not Miss Westbrooke. But to be frank', he added dismissively 'I should take no regard if it did for such matters are entirely between the persons concerned. Yet if an enmity between Mrs Ferrars and your father was presumed it might prove to be of great value to England. I came also to seek your help.Your beauty is justly praised, but I know you to also possess a quality of mind which so perfectly complements that of your friend that, were you to be left aside in what I ask, your country would be much the poorer for it.'

'Thank you for that opinion my lord', said Caroline with a cool politeness. 'I have rendered Mrs Ferrars what assistance I may and will, as I trust she knows, continue to do so. But nor can I rest until her accusers are found and brought to justice. England', Miss Westbrooke concluded with a bold and defiant look, 'must wait.'

'Should that choice require to be made I accept it' said Minto. 'Yet it is my belief you may perform both services together.'

'I fail to see how', Caroline answered, looking down and playing idly with her silver bracelet, an action signifying better than any words could have done an end to further debate. Lord Minto accordingly turned his attentions to Lucy.

'Miss Westbrooke's spirit and loyalty are very evident Mrs Ferrars. Since the work I ask of you may be dangerous such qualities between friends may also be the difference between life and death. But it could not be of more importance. So much so that one might almost say any sum might be considered by way of reward.'

'Indeed?', said Lucy, her eyes brightening at the prospect. 'Then pray be seated and tell us if you will my lord, of this matter.'

When Minto had taken a chair opposite to those occupied by the two attractive blondes he began, in a sombre tone, to address them.

'Very well ladies. You can hardly be unaware of the danger that is now threatening our shores. Bonaparte's army is assembling across the Channel. One thing and one thing alone, prevents its marching through England and that is the navy.You are acquainted with Lord Brocklehurst?'

'We have never been introduced', answered Lucy, 'but are with his wife, who resides I believe, still in York.She told us that her husband was much in Portsmouth concerned with the fleet. But we have never learned the nature of his duties.'

Minto laughed harshly. 'No Mrs Ferrars you would not, for I dare say that she knows no more than you do. Let us say then that, if Lord Nelson flies the flags and fires the cannon, then Brocklehurst kills the rats and empties out the slops. Dirty work. Very dirty work. For Bonaparte has rats in England. Who will, if they can, gnaw through the timbers of our ships before ever they set sail. So we sat there, Lord Brocklehurst and I and names of cats were mentioned. Two and both with hair the colour of ripest corn.'

'That compliment belongs to Miss Westbrooke my lord' replied Lucy, with a genuinely admiring glance at Caroline's mass of piled up tresses, 'my own being somewhat paler. However we always hunt together. What might be the work for such cats?'

'We have not been sleeping in our hammocks Mrs Ferrars', replied Minto. 'Two little pieces of vermin we have caught already and one squeaked before it died. Telling of its leader, the one by whose command all scamper scurry and bite. It wears not a uniform, but a bonnet and gown. Moves also it seems along the very best of tables.'

'Where Lord Minto? London? Portsmouth?'

'York?', ventured Caroline, looking up from her bracelet briefly. 'Or', she added, as attentions returned to it, 'perhaps here in Bath?'

Minto chuckled.

'You have chosen wisely it seems in your companion Mrs Ferrars. We got but one word, of sorts there, from our rat. It was Batork.'

Lucy looked angry and replied with matching irritation. 'Oh really my lord this will not do at all. That may mean Bath, or York, or both, or something else entirely. A pity indeed that neither Miss Westbrooke nor myself was present with some steady drops of gentle rain to soften up the ground before lifting the vessel up. For, with your heavy handed plough, you broke the pot entirely.'

Caroline again looked up. 'Might I make a guess Lord Minto that your rat was taken at the beginning of last month? At the time, or very near it, when Mrs Ferrars was also 'taken away'?

'You might Miss Westbrooke.'

'Then I can eat two meals together. If Mrs Ferrars accepts your offer.'

'I thank you for that', said Lucy with a smile to her only friend. 'We have no other help but require none. Since Miss Rebecca Frobisher and Miss Catherine de Traile, who have assisted us in our duties here, have, it would appear, now left our service. What are your terms my lord?'

'If you find the Queen Rat? Two thousand pounds for you Mrs Ferrars and the same for Miss Westbrooke. With whatever other rewards and honours his majesty and other grateful citizens may wish to bestow upon both of you. Five hundred pounds is to be handed over today. Whatever the outcome of your battle.'

'I accept the challenge', said Lucy.

'And I', added Caroline. 'How much time Lord Minto', she continued, 'do you believe we have?'

'Only Bonaparte can answer that question', said Minto handing the money over to her. 'And he is not a patient man.'

As he moved towards the door Lucy followed with a thoughtful expression. Caroline was on the far side of the room and busy counting out the downpayment when Mrs Ferrars voiced her thoughts in little more than a whisper.

'I value the faith you place in me my lord. Yet have you told us all? Have you not ladies in, or out, of society for such work. Why myself?'

Minto looked back at her as if trying to fathom all that lay behind the pretty face.

'Perhaps because you are a mystery also Mrs Ferrars. Oh to be Miss Westbrooke's friend, that I can well understand. Though I confess to being both pleased and surprised that you find more value in that than merely social advantage .But who are you? Indeed 'what' are you? We could find in Devon not even sure proof of your existence. One might almost suppose you to be a spirit. An invention of the mind. Transported to these perilous times by some power beyond our understanding to serve your country's needs. Above all things an enemy fears what is beyond his comprehension.

'Or beyond her comprehension my lord?'

'Quite so Mrs Ferrars', said Minto, shutting the door behind him.

CHAPTER TWO

' GOLD AND SILVER'

'Well. Where shall we begin? What, did you fashion out of that word Batork?'

'Mmmm. If it is a marriage', began Miss Westbrooke thoughtfully in answer to Lucy's question, 'of the cities of Bath and York then do both contain rats or have they moved? Did the man change from the one to the other to throw us off the scent or was he revealing the truth? I suppose if he was in some pain, through torture, the second is more likely.'

Lucy nodded. 'Yes I would agree with that. But there is also another possibility. That, at present, he does not know where the Queen Rat resides. She may even have a house in both. More likely however is that only those in her immediate circle are privy to her exact movements. I dare say Lord Minto's men have but fished up a sprat.'

Mrs Ferrars paused in her reflections to look at her companion and evaluate her role in the trials ahead. It would be virtually impossible for Caroline Westbrooke's wits to equal her looks of course, but they would never be shamed either in such company as so many still foolishly chose to believe. Hopefully the mistake would continue to be made too. Noting the look Caroline gave a merry laugh.

'I can guess your thoughts', she said teasingly.

'Can you?' answered Lucy with a challenging smile.

'Yes. You are always pleased when I use my head! But tell me that you like my dress also!'

'Of course I do. In fact I consider it to be one of your prettiest.'

'Thank you. I am pleased at that, for so do I. I know your fondness for white and so decided against the green sarsenet hoping that we might be alike today. As, indeed, we are! Oh well! I am a total slave to clothes! Why should I wish to deny it? You must find my passion of annoyance sometimes, though never once have you said so. Sweetest Lucy!', added Miss Westbrooke sitting down on the sofa and beckoning for Mrs Ferrars to do likewise. 'Now tell me true. Is my 'passion' ever such an irritation to you?'

'I can assure you that it is not. Indeed I shall encourage you to talk still more of gowns, bonnets, boots and pelisses. Especially in company.'

'I shall require no invitation to do that!', answered Caroline, 'but now', she added a little more seriously, leaning across to pick up some papers from a side table, 'I have something I wish to show you. It is my record of some arrivals in our city of Bath. Let me see, ah yes, here are the entries since the third of this month.'

What Lucy saw first was a list. Miss Caroline Westbrooke took as much painstaking pride in her writing as she did in music, dancing, sketching and fashion and, in their investigations , Lucy had on more than one occasion, good reason to bless that meticulous attention to neatness and detail.So she read with great attention, as I urge the reader to do, first the aforementioned list and then Caroline's observations upon it.

The third.   Miss Louisa Blandford and Mrs Hunter.

The fifth.   Miss Charlotte Cantlemere (returned from Bristol).

The sixth.   Countess Marie Barbazon. Monsieur Charles Barbazon. Mademoiselle Catherine Barbazon.

The eighth.   Duke Robert Lavalle. Duchess Louise Lavalle. Mademoiselle Lucie Lavalle.

Mrs Hunter. Sour in conversation and yet more so in manner. Not unpleasing in appearance and might even have a certain elegance were she not to attempt to wear pink which she cannot do to satisfaction.

Miss Louisa Blandford. Aged seventeen years and of pleasing appearance. Have nothing to say against her other than that she was in Mrs Hunter's company for which she cannot justly be blamed. We were introduced not until the ninth, but before we parted, and in the company of Mademoiselle Lavalle who seemed by her expression to share the sentiment, she greatly praised my hair. I felt it only correct therefore to pay compliment to her own arrangement of short curls.Of course my own hair is so very precious that I could not possibly contemplate sacrificing it to the scissors, but, upon her, the effect was of sufficient satisfaction as to make my words honest enough. I should say from a conversation which I had with her upon the theatre that she has a good eye and sharp wits.

Miss Charlotte Cantlemere. I should hardly feel the need to write about Charlotte were it not that she brings me word that dearest Lucy, without whom, in spite of Charlotte's company, I have been quite destitute, is to return to Bath. What joy I feel at that news! Charlotte has been a great comfort, and though she is but silver to Lucy's gold, we are firm friends. Charlotte says that she has always believed in Lucy's innocence which I am inclined to believe true from her expression when speaking to me upon it.

Countess Marie Barbazon. I have yet to make the acquaintance of the countess or of her son and daughter, but look forward to doing so upon the twentieth of the month when, I hope, Lucy will be able to accompany me. Mademoiselle Catherine Barbazon is nineteen and accounted to be one of the two most handsome looking ladies in Bath. I flatter myself that opinion considers me to be the other so I have a great desire to meet her. Count Barbazon was guillotined in the year eighteen hundred.

Duke Robert Lavalle. Introduced to him at the Pump Rooms The duke, as I shall refer to him, since he is now in England and not France, was most friendly, polite, courteous, chivalrous and charming. Sadly he is married and aged oh perhaps fifty. I liked his company as much as he appeared to take pleasure in mine.

Duchess Louise Lavalle. Somewhat younger than her husband and with a careless elegance in the french fashion of things. She has a temper I should fancy, yet despite her husband's attentions to me, we conversed quite pleasantly and I could find nothing in her to dislike.

Mademoiselle Lucie Lavalle. I made mention of her before in connection with Miss Blandford. The young lady is of a similar age and the two have, it would appear, formed something of a friendship. Miss Lucie is of a dark and delicate prettiness with a decidedly lively air and she talked a little with me of dancing at which I understand from her mother she excels. I liked her manners, indeed she was, with her quite good english, most amiable. I wonder what my Lucy will fashion out of the one who bears her name in french?

When she had finished reading Lucy Ferrars put down the papers and grasped Caroline's hands firmly in hers.

'Those are my thoughts' said Miss Westbrooke softly 'for what they may be worth. Though I know you place little value on sensibilities.'

'Well', answered Lucy,'I am as well acquainted with deception and malice as any and make no apology for it. The world is a hard place and one may use any weapon to cut a way through. I was not born rich as you know and had to climb up little by little.'

'Miss Lucy Steele', replied Caroline as if she was delivering a speech or tribute to an audience rather than taking part in a one to one private conversation, 'has an elder sister by name Anne, who is decidedly plain and not at all accomplished. Lucy however by contrast is both pretty and smart. She is engaged to Mr Edward Ferrars, but this does not meet with the approval of his family and, when the secret is out, he is disinherited, becoming instead a clergyman of limited means who marries one Miss Dashwood with whom he is in love. Lucy meantime marries Mr Edward's younger brother Robert who has fine prospects. The marriage not proving an especially happy one to either party sees her, with the full consent and support of her husband, take up rooms in Bath where she makes the acquaintance of Miss Caroline Westbrooke whom later, by her wits, she saves from a hanging. So much does her fame spread that Mrs Ferrars' aid is sought by many thereafter and she becomes wealthy, moving amongst the very best in society. Have I neglected anything?'

'Your own importance' answered Lucy very seriously. 'For I could not have risen so high so quick without you. I shall never forget that. If you felt you ever owed a debt it has been repaid now. It is not just for freedom neither. While I cannot quite allow myself to have been destitute, I truly am very pleased indeed to see you again my dear Caroline.'

Miss Westbrooke smiled tenderly and put her arm round Lucy's waist. Suddenly, with that spontaneously affectionate gesture, Mrs Ferrars, for ever watchful, felt very very tired and, without realising, relaxed so far as to let her head fall onto her friend's shoulder.

What was it she had said?, Caroline mused dreamily as they sat there side by side. 'I shall never forget that'. Yes that was it. 'No you will not' pondered Miss Westbrooke as she also fell to sleep. Others might. But she would not. Mrs Lucy Ferrars. Miss Lucy Steele that was. She would not.

CHAPTER THREE

'FISHING IN A DARK POOL'

Not at all to Miss Westbrooke's surprise all those that she had made careful notes upon were present at the Assembly Rooms the following evening. Along of course, with many others.One above all was a most familiar face and, their differences having now been resolved, was the most envied gentleman in Bath with Caroline on his arm. Mrs Lucy Ferrars walked alongside.

'Well George. When are you going to get this girl of yours married off? High time now you know', said the bluff Lady Mary Cantlemere, the mother of Caroline's friend Charlotte. Nor was her blunt remark without an edge to it. Young women, she considered, had far too much say in their lives these days and would not be told what to do. Her own daughter, since she had befriended Miss Westbrooke, was one of the worst. Though not quite the worst. There was no doubt who qualified for that title.

'I am not yours to command Lady Cantlemere', answered Caroline boldly and looking her straight in the eye. 'Indeed', she added with a complacent smile, 'I may well decide not to marry at all.'

'All heiresses must marry Miss Westbrooke. I am afraid you will be given no choice.'

Caroline's expression looked as if she had just smelled something very unpleasant.To be quizzed by Charlotte's insufferable mother was intolerable. It should not be borne. It would not be borne.

'You presume to know me very well.'

Mary seemed more amused than annoyed by Caroline's superior and icy tone.

'I know your circumstances that is all.'

A little taken aback, Miss Caroline Westbrooke looked quickly at her father. Seeing that anxious look and the angry defiance that it also betrayed, Viscount Westbrooke too, became cold in his response.

'My daughter's wishes will be honoured.'

'Yes of course', replied Mary Cantlemere with just the kind of smile to Caroline that made Miss Westbrooke want to slap her in the face. 'A marriage without harmony may be most injurious for a woman. What do you think Mrs Ferrars?'

'Do you speak from experience of such Lady Cantlemere?', answered Lucy with such a look of sugary sympathy as to make Mary now want to hand out the slaps.'My own has neither true harmony nor true misery to it and I dare say my husband would say the same.'

'I have heard of you madam. From my friend Lady Susan Fortescue.'

'Oh Lady Fortescue', replied Lucy casually. 'Is she here in Bath? I should indeed welcome a further meeting with her. But not half so much I dare say as Miss Westbrooke would. If I recollect correctly', continued Lucy slowly her eyes narrowing, 'she made my friend', (and Lucy heavily emphasised that 'my'),'a little present and then entrusted the giving of it to another. How much thought and trouble that involved. I have yet to fully repay her for it.'

'I shall inform Lady Fortescue of your request', said Mary Cantlemere as she turned away.'She is at present in London. You may meet again in less pleasant circumstances there. Bonaparte's army is poised for invasion.Should he succeed in crossing the water we shall need all our friends shall we not?'

'Friends? Of course', answered Mrs Ferrars to Mary's retreating back.

'I had heard that Susan Fortescue was in London' said Viscount Westbrooke. 'I had also heard', he continued lowering his voice, 'that she holds little love for my Caroline and less still for her closest friend.'

Lucy laughed harshly. 'She has good reason for her dislike of me. However she probably does not realise the depth of mine for her, for it has festered nicely. Lady Fortescue you see my lord is a common enough sort of cunning woman whose cup of malice only true fills up when her own fortunes empty and, in consequence, believe all others of her sex to be like her. My own malicious intent can be ridden as well on a winning horse as upon a losing one. As to her dislike of your daughter envy of a sweet and affectionate nature, a richer mix of accomplishments and, most of all, when she takes a long look in her own mirror of a morning are all the answers there.'

'It is two years since our last meeting with her', added Caroline, after acknowledging Lucy Ferrars words with a little smile.'One might well suppose that she has been trying to run away from us. But now, if you will forgive me', she continued to her father and leaving his side to link arms with Lucy, 'I should wish to take a turn about the room with Mrs Ferrars.'

'Of course my dear' replied the Viscount and off he went in search of both a drink and male company.

When, in circulating, Caroline and Lucy were introduced to the Barbazons, Miss Westbrooke considered that gossip had in no way exaggerated the remarkable attractiveness of Mademoiselle Catherine. Caroline was perhaps two inches taller, her hair was golden and not auburn and her eyes green, not brown. But, as the gentlemen looked from one white gowned goddess to the other, all was brilliant beauty.Observant ladies took a different tack. Would these society Venuses, eyeing each other carefully, be friends or not? Many, purely for their own amusement, trusted it might be the latter.

'Bath ees so vayree playsant', said Countess Marie Barbazon in heavily accented english, 'yet it too it cannot escape - yes - what ees corming.'

'And what, pray, is that Countess?', asked Caroline pointedly.

'Wahr Mademoiselle Waystbrook.'

'Oh I hardly think so', said Caroline. 'Bonaparte may have a fine army, but he must get his men across the Channel. Unless they be fine swimmers at dead of night we are in little danger. The french navy is no match for ours.'

Monsieur Charles Barbazon, Catherine's brother, who had arrived in Bath from London only that day, looked hard at her. 'You speak wisely mademoiselle. But can you be so certain that your fleet will ever set sail?'

'Whatever do you mean sir?'

'A door Mademoiselle Westbrooke, it may be opened from the inside also', he replied with a slow and knowing smile.

'Not if the key is first taken by another', suggested Lucy Ferrars gently.

Charles Barbazon, the smile now quite gone, looked hard at her. But before he had chance to make any reply his sister turned to Caroline.

'Your gown mademoiselle. Excuse moi. C'est tres jolie. Magnifique.'

'Merci mademoiselle', answered Caroline, hitting the conversational ball back with an identical shot. 'Yours is also.. oh pardon.. tres belle!'

In spite of Catherine's halting english and Caroline's far from accomplished french (an uncharacteristic laziness in her schoolgirl studies that some readers may recall from previous adventures), both ladies were astute enough to recognise a genuine compliment from a pretence at one and exchanged cautious smiles.Thus,for the time being at least, many of the watching women were set to be disappointed in their hopes.

Introductions for and to Lucy were then made with others, firstly to Miss Louisa Blandford and her chaperone Mrs Hunter and then to the Lavalles. In this party of five Miss Louisa, though reserved, was friendly and polite, but Eleanor Hunter did nothing either in limited speech or still more limited manners to make Lucy question Caroline's assessment. Duke Robert Lavalle's attentions to Miss Westbrooke took up most of his time, but to Mrs Ferrars he was pleasant and if his wife was merely coolly polite, the daughter proved more genial. Mademoiselle Lucie also proved most respectful and when Caroline in a whispered aside, informed her that Mrs Ferrars shared her christian name it seemed to cause the young woman a high degree of pleasure.

'You are acquainted with many here mademoiselle?' said Lucy to her namesake as Caroline, making up a little circle of four, turned to talk with Louisa Blandford.

'Some Lady Ferrars', replied Lucie Lavalle and Lucy smiled at the leap in her status. Without feeling the least need to correct the error.

'Indeed?'

'Yes. Les Barbazons.'

'Les Barbazons?'

Lucy Ferrars looked across at Duchess Lavalle who had overheard her daughter's words and, 'question like', repeated them.

'Yes', tempted Lucy with a disarmingly innocent look.

'Take your, how you say, care. Mademoiselle Catherine I do not know. But ze others. Take your care.'

'You must understand Lady Ferrars' said Lucie Lavalle, 'that not all the families en.. in.. France, lost everything.'

'Do I understand mademoiselle that the Barbazons did not?'

'You speak of our enemies Madame.'

Lucy turned to look at Duke Robert, standing next to his wife. In those steady eyes she saw a courteous admiration, but also an air of perplexity.

'How so my lord duke?'

'Christophe Barbazon, the cousin of that Catherine so much admired , is a captain in the army of Bonaparte. It is my understand, understanding, that Monsieur has not been in Paris for some time. May I, forgive me Madame Ferrars, speak alone with Mademoiselle Westbrooke? It is - important.'

Caroline smiled and made a forward motion with her hand. It was an open gesture of assent that seemed to annoy both the duchess and Mrs Hunter who promptly walked off together in the opposite direction. After Lucie Lavalle and Louisa Blandford had also made their departures Mrs Ferrars was left alone. But not for long.

'Keep your wits about you tonight. And read this.'

Lucy looked up to see Lord Minto passing her quickly by and felt a piece of paper thrust into her left hand. She looked around and, seeing a convenient pillar ten paces distant with no one near it, a nonchalant walk around the same was more than sufficient to read her correspondence.Which was the following.

Hounds loose. To H6314 end.

'Will you please follow me ma'am.'

Lucy looked at the maidservant standing three or four feet away. A pretty round red faced girl about seventeen she supposed. Mrs Ferrars nodded and, stepping finally outside, found herself again in the company of Lord Minto who motioned first her into the waiting carriage and then, as he followed, told the coachman to drive off.

'Do not be alarmed madam.'

'I am not my lord.'

Minto gave a thin smile. 'You read it?'

'I did.'

'Your thoughts?'

'I assume Miss Westbrooke and myself to be the hounds and that the H six three one four is the place to which they, whosoever 'they' may be, will go.'

'And the 'end?''

'I cannot think that is where our quest will finish. Most like it is of relation to what has gone before. Perhaps a place mentioned in a book or newspaper.'

Minto clapped his hands and began slowly to speak.

'Off with his head and set it on York gates.

So York may overlook the town of York.'

'My lord?' asked Lucy a little puzzled.

'A speech made by Queen Margaret Mrs Ferrars. In Shakespeare's play King Henry the Sixth. Part Three.'

Lucy nodded, adding with a wry grin, 'No doubt at the very end of Act One Scene Four' and Minto matched the nod.

'Yet there may be more than that', he replied. 'Oh perhaps it is just fancy. But Queen Margaret was french, the duke was her enemy and a duke's head was cut off and indeed put above that gateway into York.'

'Where and when was that piece of paper found Lord Minto?'

'Good questions Mrs Ferrars. England's money is not being wasted. It was discovered... well..'

'Yes my lord?'

'Discovered', continued Minto, his expression unfathomable, 'in Mademoiselle Lucie Lavalle's reticule.'

'By you?'

'No.'

'Then how may you be sure?'

'I cannot. Only Mademoiselle Lavalle can be certain of that. For it was she who gave it me.'

'I see. And as to the when?'

'That is what seems so curious. She is most insistent that it could not have been there when she last opened the bag.'

'Which was?'

'As she observed Miss Westbrooke and yourself approach. So you see Mrs Ferrars, if the girl speaks true, only four other people could have placed it there.'

'To know that my lord', quizzed Lucy, 'you must yourself have observed the whole time our conversation and what passed before it. Yet you saw nothing?'

'I did not. I was standing a little way behind this pillar. Mademoiselle Lavalle could be lying. Yet.'

'Just so. For much of the time her conversation was devoted to myself. Moreover I fancy I am quite observant by nature and not easy deceived. One cannot be firm of course but I should not have supposed her either cunning or malicious. However I take it that we must now, with our country's blessing, set out for York?'

'You do Mrs Ferrars. You will need friends there. Two carriages will depart tomorrow at eleven. Miss Westbrooke and yourself will be collected at a half past by her father and Miss Cantlemere will also accompany you for it seems that she is to pay a visit to her aunt who resides in that city. I shall travel in the second carriage close behind with two soldiers of the militia. Both coachmen will also be armed as will a companion beside them.'

'It appears my lord', said Lucy carefully, 'that I must trust you.'

'We must trust each other' said Minto as the carriage once more drew up at the Assembly Rooms and the two of them alighted. 'For the sake of England.'

CHAPTER FOUR

'ARRIVALS AT YORK'

On the journey northward Viscount Westbrooke and Mrs Ferrars were largely silent. For Charlotte and Caroline were, for a great deal of the time, talking fashion. Actually Miss Cantlemere was doing most of the talking with Caroline, to Lucy's inward amusement, only interrupting her from time to time with factual accuracy rather than personal opinions. Even granted Charlotte's fondness for her own voice it was surprising that the conversation was so one way. After all Miss Westbrooke and clothes was almost a saying in itself. But Caroline had been thoughtful ever since her brief conversation the previous evening with Duke Robert Lavalle. He had begged her to remain in Bath.' You must' he stated, 'for only death is your reward if you do not.'

Upon their arrival in the city there was soon a parting of the ways as Charlotte, met by her aunt Mrs Andrews, moved on to the latter's house on Micklegate while the remainder of the party settled into rooms at the 'White Swan'. The following day however, when all were gathered in Mrs Andrews' drawing room, saw Caroline float an idea in general conversation.

'We must pay a call upon the new Countess Arcachon.'

'An excellent notion my dear' said her father. 'Though Lord Minto and myself have other matters to attend to I am sure that she would welcome it.'

'I also must decline' said Mrs Andrews, 'but as for you Charlotte it is a fine idea.'   .

Lucy wondered quite what emotions this proposed meeting might arouse. Readers with knowledge of previous investigations may recall the name of Miss Isabella Lunsford of Dufton Park.It was she who was this Countess. At one time Isabella and Caroline might have been considered rivals, since good looks and fine breeding, not to mention a wealthy inheritance, made each a heady mix for suitors. That was very different now, not only due to Isabella's married status, but also, before they had parted company last year, a mutual respect and even an admiration for each other's qualities. No, Lucy's slant was quite a different one. How would Charlotte Cantlemere be viewed?

Since being in York almost two days Charlotte had hardly addressed a word to Lucy. She was not unpleasant in the few that had been spoken, but Mrs Ferrars was in little doubt that that was entirely due to the fact that both enjoyed Caroline's friendship. Charlotte was attractive enough in her way, with dark brown eyes and hair complementing a slim tall figure. In addition she was also, though her elder brother was married and would inherit the family estate, worth a cool 20,000 pounds to any man who could catch her.but such a task would be well beyond many for Miss Cantlemere judged people largely upon the question of high birth. She was heartily detested by the maids, for harsh words could wound, especially when accompanied by the not infrequent dismissal. Social inferiors were there, in Charlotte's thinking, either to be made use of or ignored. Nor was she liked by many of her peers. To men she was sneering and waspish, to women of her own age cold, critical and arrogant. Yet in spite of all this it did appear that Charlotte Cantlemere had some affection for Caroline Westbrooke. Lucy had found no reason so far to doubt that, and, until evidence appeared to the contrary, would continue to regard Caroline as the exception to a general unflattering rule.

The request was quickly made and still more quickly accepted. The following afternoon, battlelines were drawn early as Charlotte and Isabella eyed up each others gowns.

'I understand you are all residing at 'The White Swan' Mrs Ferrars?', said Countess Isabella Arcachon. 'I should be most willing for you all to be my guests during your stay in York.'

'Thank you no', replied Lucy.'We must, I fancy, remain in the city. There is a matter which drew me here that cannot allow for the pleasures of either your company or a country estate and Miss Westbrooke must also be so denied. However Miss Cantlemere may wish to accept.'

'To come to York and bury myself in the country?', said Charlotte scornfully, presenting in order a screwed up face to Caroline and a smilingly superior one to Lucy and Isabella. 'What, pray, might I do? Tend cows or grow vegetables? I should surely become one or the other.'

'Oh the country has its own charms', intervened Caroline. 'But being so long in London and Bath you cannot be so well aware of them as I. Were circumstances otherwise I should be delighted to stay here.Especially with such a hostess.'

'But I should be deprived of your company', replied Charlotte, touching Caroline's arm.

'You are quite right Miss Cantlemere', said Isabella carefully looking straight at her. ' Value what you have. Miss Westbrooke makes friends easily, but not everyone can be so fortunate. Shall we take tea?'

Until that beverage was brought the four ladies contented themselves with standard conversational pleasantries upon the weather and the fine prospect (which even Charlotte was forced to admit), of the grounds to be viewed through the window. However, once some sips had been taken, Lucy began her own schedule of gossip.

'Your husband is away at present Countess?'

'Yes. Indeed, since our marriage four months past I have seen him but little. Philippe has much pressing business in the capital. I expect him to return here in the autumn.The animals miss him, for he seems partial to them all, especially the horses. But when London shouts he listens.'

'I see' said Lucy.

'London is not at all pleasant in the summer months', suggested Charlotte. 'I should imagine that the Count will be most pleased to return. Indeed, upon a fine day and viewing as I now do, the grounds here, his business, especially with a new bride, must surely be of the highest importance to keep him from the north.'

Lucy and Isabella looked simultaneously at the speaker for the snide smile, but on the face of it the remark was an honest one. Countess Arcachon gave a little forward movement of her head, looking directly now into Charlotte's eyes as she replied.

'Miss Cantlemere you speak my own thoughts. It encourages also servants tales and that is most unwelcome. Indeed I was forced to dismiss my lady's maid, Belinda, on that very matter only last week.'

'I have been considering', said Charlotte, studying an apparently still vexed Isabella. 'I do fear that I have done the country something of an injustice after all Countess. So, if you will graciously consent to accept my pardon I should be most pleased to be your guest here.'

'You will be most welcome Miss Cantlemere. Be assured that Mrs Ferrars and Miss Westbrooke will be frequent visitors. I shall not permit refusal.'

'When circumstances allow we shall certainly avail ourselves of your hospitality' said Caroline with a forgiving smile to Charlotte, who did indeed seem a little uncomfortable with her apparent change of heart. 'I am sure that you will find each other most interesting company.'

The following late morning saw Miss Charlotte Cantlemere, with the inevitable impressive retinue of fashionable clothes, set out for Dufton Park. Accompanied for the day and dinner beyond it, by Caroline and Lucy. For Mrs Ferrars was keen to gain information and, while Charlotte was being shown to her room, promptly made her first efforts. Which bore fruit faster than she could have expected.

'You ask for names of visitors I can recollect coming recently to York' said Isabella. 'Well I fancy I can do better still. For I have kept my own written account. Here it is. I know Mrs Lucy Ferrars and Miss Caroline Westbrooke do not spend their moments idly.'

Mrs Ferrars nodded and taking the piece of paper which was now thrust into her hand, proceeded to put it in her reticule.It remained there until, after an hour long coach journey back to their rooms at the 'White Swan' and a promise to return to Dufton Park the following afternoon for evening dinner, Lucy and Caroline began to read its contents.

ARRIVALS AT YORK.

Miss Eleanor Stott. Unremarkable in all save a general modesty. Of a quiet and serious disposition. Aged twenty and one. Arrived from Newcastle with her sister Catherine and her aunt Mrs Poyning. Miss Catherine is prettier than her sister.

Mr John Saxby, from the nearby country estate of Hoverham, gives me a great wish to be no longer married. He is charming and a great wit. Unmarried, a state in him which every woman likewise hereabouts seems determined to alter to her own pleasure and advantage. His sister Miss Louisa is seventeen and has an artful knowing manner which reminds me greatly of a past acquaintance. I noted that she had a long conversation in french with Miss Catherine Stott with Mrs Jane Saxby watchful beside them.

The Fullers have also arrived. Mr Thomas is as bold and remarkably handsome as ever and it is said that he considers Countess Arcachon the finest of her sex. His brother, who has been in London of late, is less forthcoming but even so more than Miss Belinda their sister.

'Well Caroline', said Lucy looking up. 'With the excellent work that you have done in Bath these thoughts of Isabella Arcachon, though not of your clarity, will also be of value to us. We must find a pattern to follow Queen Rat to her hiding place. But for now there is little we can accomplish other than devoting ourselves to dinner. Thoughts without information upon which to hang them are fruitless Do you not agree?'

'In the main yes. But we have something of use. Many speak french. Some are french. Our danger is french.'

'My meaning exactly. To speak french well is no grounds for guilt, nor to speak it ill sure grounds for innocence. As to being french your thoughts, with respect, are still less of value. For many seek refuge here from the very Bonaparte that we seek to destroy. Still', Lucy concluded thoughtfully and patting Caroline's hand, 'to make a chain you do need to fashion links and that is more than I has managed. Is that all your thoughts?'

'Not entirely,but my other is of still less note. I wonder only how Isabella and Charlotte are fighting their battles of muslins and sarsenets! There! I told you it was of little value.'

'Perhaps', replied Mrs Ferrars.

On arriving at Dufton Park the next day Lucy and Caroline were startled to see a great scurrying of servants at the gateway and, no sooner had they alighted from their carriage than Isabella Arcachon ran up to greet them.

'Thank goodness you have come! We have had such happenings here.'

'Pray be calm', said Caroline Westbrooke, drawing the mistress of Dufton to one side away from the servants, 'and tell us.'

'Your friend Miss Cantlemere is nowhere to be found. We ate at one, shortly after she retired to her room and since then has not been seen. A carriage did depart in some haste, but none of the servants can recall anyone step inside it. Two of my ostlers, John and Michael, whom I have never found to be false, will say the same as I.'

'There is something else you have to tell us is there not?' said Lucy. 'For I saw the look upon your face. Miss Cantlemere's sudden disappearance might cause you much concern and even distress. But not fear. What is it ?'

'I shall show you' replied Isabella and they followed her into the hallway.There, lying just inside the entrance doorway was something covered over by a dark cloak.

'The carriage drew up, this bundle was thrown out and then the carriage went away again. One of my ostlers began to give chase but..'

'Yes?' prompted Lucy.

'He stopped. A shot was fired through the carriage window grazing his arm and John...'

'Very wisely decided that the second shot might be more accurate than the first', said Mrs Ferrars.

As Isabella nodded Lucy removed the cloak and looked at its contents. A severed hand is never a pretty sight.

But yet more distressing when the distinctive rings upon it were those of the vanished Miss Rebecca Frobisher.

CHAPTER FIVE

'THE REBECCA STONE'

Even Lucy was shocked at the sight and as for Caroline, who had befriended the girl almost two years ago, it was some minutes before the flood of tears ceased. When they were there was a look of such bitter anger as Mrs Ferrars had never seen before upon Miss Westbrooke's face.

'I want to know who has done this. And when I do let them face me, not the hangman.'

'Can you use a sword?' asked Isabella in answer to Caroline's words. 'For I can instruct you if you wish.'

'My father taught me to fire a pistol.'

'I see. And you Mrs Ferrars?'

'I have merely observed both accomplishments. Nor can I easy imagine Miss Westbrooke displaying much enthusiasm.'

'I hate to kill anything it is true', Caroline responded. 'When I was but twelve my father gave me a loaded gun to shoot at a poor crow. I took care to miss my aim and the bird took flight. He laughed rather than scolded me for the action and all my practice thereafter was devoted to pieces of wood. But I am certain I could take the life that ended sweet Rebecca's.'

'Then we are not so very different' said Isabella. 'I do not kill for pleasure either. Though I could pluck a pigeon or a partridge as well as any cook if I had to.'

'And do you fight, -forgive me- in your gown?' The idea evidently was not one the very appearance conscious Miss Westbrooke accepted at all lightly.

'Well certainly not in this one' said Isabella and the three women managed just the semblance of smiles. 'But yes. I have duelled, in play naturally, nine times here and all with gentlemen. My first encounter was with my cousin. Which I lost. You remember him I dare say? Frederick, the husband of her that was Miss Anne Standish. Who is very near her time.'

'So we understand', replied Caroline, 'else we should have called at Grant House upon her already.'

'Well I am certain when the child is born', Isabella said positively, 'that the new mother will then wish for no better company than yourselves.'

'That is a kind thought and especially now at such a sad time. But what of your other duels?'

'Shall we say' replied Isabella to Caroline's question, 'that had they been to the death I should still be alive.'

A knock at the door stopped any further discussion as a footman approached Countess Isabella Arcachon.

'Beg pardon your ladyship. But John, the gardener, found this upon the step. He felt that you should see it.'

Isabella nodded and took the piece of paper from the man. He was about to leave until Lucy, with a quick motion of her left hand, indicated that he stop.

'A moment. This paper. You say it was found upon the step. When?'

'John noticed it beside the body ma'am. It was placed under a small stone he said. His exact words ma'am.'

'Well it was not there when the Countess, Miss Westbrooke and myself arrived. So it would seem that he took it before. Why I wonder?'

'He says so that no one else might take it ma'am. Intending then to inform the Countess of it.'

'A likely tale!' said Isabella. 'No doubt he thought it money, or, perhaps, that he might obtain other advantages from its contents. You may leave us' she added loftily to the footman. 'I shall speak to the gardener later.'

When he had left Lucy shook her head. 'I fancy you judge too harshly. If the man found that there was no money to be had why not just throw it away? Or, if he felt there might be, why tell others of his discovery?'

'And then' added Caroline, 'he must have known that we would be likely to quiz him and that his motives would be questioned. Has he been at the estate long?'

'Since before my father's time. John was a trusted head gardener then. I have often heard my late father say so.'

'I should not have supposed a good opinion from such a source easy to obtain?', said Caroline, 'therefore he has not only nothing to gain, but also much to lose. I should say he speaks the truth.'

Lucy nodded. 'I am sure Miss Westbrooke is right. What does the paper say?'

Having read it a fogged and somewhat irritated Countess passed the communication across with a shrug of the shoulders.

'Perhaps John is loyal and that is a reassurance. Yet his honesty is hardly worth such pains for nonsense.'

Lucy Ferrars read for herself. Certainly they were words not only not to be found in Doctor Johnson's Dictionary, but not in any other either this side of the moon.

pnl nnp lppnnlo. pnonlanel llpo al onaelo.

Having passed the 'nonsense' across for Caroline's perusal Lucy had a great desire to see the finely worked firescreen at the far end of the room and requested that the Countess accompany her to explain the workmanship. Letting her eyes wander, but not her mind. After a minute or so she turned about, but, before anyone had the opportunity to be either open or closed on any of their their reflections a maidservant arrived with a message for Isabella. Having read it Countess Arcachon looked up with a smile.

'It is from my cousin Frederick at Grant House. The message is in three parts. Firstly he welcomes you both to York and secondly insists that you now reside with them during your time here unless you make strong objection. He says this especially upon his wife's account, for she is most eager to meet with you both again.'

'Of course we shall', said Caroline.

'I am also agreeable to that' added Lucy. 'But you spoke of three parts to the message. Is there then an introduction to make?'

'Indeed there is. Lady Lunsford is delivered of a baby daughter', pronounced Isabella triumphantly.

When later that evening the two ladies from Bath had returned to their rooms and sent off 'post haste' their acceptance of Lord Frederick's offer, they turned their attentions to the mysterious note which Caroline had taken the opportunity, at the writing desk, to make a copy of.

'I guessed your ruse with the firescreen of course', said Miss Westbrooke. 'But I see from your face that you have made a beginning where I have not. Come Lucy! What water has been drawn up from this well?'

Mrs Ferrars gave a dismissive wave of the hand. 'Only the obvious. The piece of paper is torn, but is folded in four and most neat done. John the gardener also said that he found it placed under a small stone .'Placed' I make mention of especially.The letters are formed carefully, each is quite clear and distinctive. So we have here a hidden message, which must be both found and cannot be misunderstood. Each letter you see must be read correctly.'

'What are you about then with your scribbles?'

'Well, as you say I have made a beginning', replied Mrs Ferrars as her companion drew up a chair alongside. 'Of course each of these letters must match with one in the correct order. But only the following are used in the message, a,e,l,n, o and p. That suggests to me that one, or two, words are used as a match and that the same words are then repeated. For example', added Lucy, 'if the words Caroline Westbrooke were used a would correspond to C , b to a, c to r and so forth. Caroline Westbrooke is- let me see now - eighteen letters long. So that, when the nineteenth letter in the alphabet is reached, one must then return to the 'C' of Caroline. Thus a and s are C, b and t are a.You see the pattern?'

Caroline, looking quickly in turn from the paper to Lucy's face and back again, nodded.

'We have two sentences here', continued Mrs Ferrars. 'The first consists of three words and the second four. In the first sentence the first and second words are short. It occurs to me that the last letter of that first word might be an 'e'. Many words with three letters end so, though, I grant, there is others that do not! If it is an 'e' one might expect it also to be found several times more in a message and so it is here, for the letter 'l' appears six times. What might that first word most like be? Come then. What is your choice?'

'The' or, possibly, 'she'.'

Lucy smiled. 'Both are good offers. For what it may be worth, since the message was found near to that bundle and its horrid contents and given that we are also ladies, I am a little the more of the second suggestion.However the next word, whether 'the' or 'she' is the horse before it, is, I dare say,a statement of some sort. Followed by an action. So we might have 'She has'.You agree?'

'Yes.'

'Very well. We shall leave that first letter for now, but ,if our other deliberations are correct, n corresponds both to the letters h and a. This means then n is both the first and eighth letter of our hidden word or words Likewise l, whether it be the or she, must match to the letter e and is fifth in the sequence.'

'Oh you clever thing', said Miss Westbrooke admiringly adding, when she had pulled up her chair a little closer, 'do please continue Lucy.'

'Now we must take a chance', Lucy Ferrars added as Miss Westbrooke both looked at and listened to her very intently. 'If our 'has' is right then p will become the letter s.That will of course fashion that first word into 'she', but also, and of equal if not more importance, possibly mean that we are repeating the pattern.'

'I would think that very likely', said Caroline, 'for few words, or even names, are longer than my own. What is more, if I am counting aright, s is the nineteenth letter and so it would be placed third on a repeated word of eight letters Making p the third letter of the hidden word. But such is only one road of many', she tailed off uncertainly and blushed, now feeling a little foolish.

'I am always happy to let my wits accompany yours on any road' replied Lucy so confidently that her friend's doubts vanished even faster than they had arrived, 'and so let us consider the longer third word. What letters have we here?'

'lppnnlo. Now let me see' said Caroline picking up the pen with fresh enthusiasm, 'that would mean that if l was the letter e- and it might well be for it occurs twice does it not- then o must be a d? For this word will represent an action of some kind. She has..oh 'something something somethinged. I am sorry. But I do find it hard at present to think beyond Rebecca.'

'I know' said Lucy taking a tearful Caroline's hand. 'But we must. For her sake too. Whatever has happened. I fancy you are right with your 'somethinged', but if the letter d is represented by o we have an answer ready. a is n, Letter one. s is p. Letter three. d is o. Letter four.h is n. Letter eight. And if..'

'Napoleon!' exclaimed Caroline triumphantly, even managing a little smile.

'Just so. So let us walk down your road and see if we may can make sense of the rest of the mystery', replied Lucy, pleased to see her friend's spirits picking up.

After a few minutes of deliberations the two women looked up at each other very seriously.For, whether a warning or a threat, the words seemed to indicate a lot more than what Countess Isabella Arcachon had called nonsense. It read, in case the reader has not followed in Lucy and Caroline's wake, as follows.

She has escaped. Catherine must be warned.

CHAPTER SIX

'THE ANGEL OF DEATH'

In spite of the pressing nature of their work both ladies were resolved to spend the next few days with Lord Frederick and Lady Anne Lunsford. Nor did Mrs Ferrars consider that a dereliction of their duties for, as she observed to Miss Westbrooke, 'Anne's knowledge of gossip hereabouts is as good as Isabella Arcachon's I fancy and, being resident in York, and thus privy to servants speculations, may carry even greater weight.'

However a communication from Dufton Park upon the morning of only their second day at Grant House meant a rapid rethink. It was written in a seemingly hurried hand.

Mrs Ferrars and Miss Westbrooke. Please come at once.

Countess Arcachon.

'Of course you must go', said Lady Lunsford, holding her baby daughter whom, to Miss Westbrooke's great surprise and delight, Anne and her husband had decided to name Caroline.

Lucy and her friend had hardly time to get inside the doorway at Dufton when Isabella, with a very set face, ushered them into the drawing room. There, placed upon the small table, was a human skull and tied, rather ludicrously upon it, a bonnet.

'You will understand', said Isabella pointedly, 'that I am just a little concerned.That was discovered by a servant this morning in an unused part of the house.'

Lucy looked at her, admiring the self control, but seeing also, in the eyes, the fear that it masked.

'What a pity it is that I was not present to meet the one who brought you such a strange gift', said Mrs Ferrars thoughtfully, 'for that would have gave me such pleasure. But tell me pray', she continued, 'from where it was found is it possible to reach the grounds without being easy seen?'

'Yes I suppose so', answered Isabella, 'for the passageway onto which all those rooms open leads from one side to the other.'

Mrs Ferrars had, when she chose to employ it, a dry and caustic wit and this, combined with Caroline Westbrooke's sympathetic support, did much to lighten the atmosphere. Yet, upon the very first night the visitors spent at Dufton, an extraordinary event took place that swallowed up all other emotions.

Caroline was sleeping in what was familiarly known as 'The Blue Room', which was particularly private, since Lucy's quarters, separated from it by an adjoining side door, provided the only access to the central passageway. Suddenly Mrs Ferrars awoke to a loud sound. Moments later her friend flung open the intervening door and sat down upon the bed frantically shaking Lucy's arm.

With a look which can only be described as terror all that Caroline could manage was pointing back with her right forefinger at the peril she had left. Next came an insistent loud knock upon the door.

Motioning Caroline to stay behind the frontline Lucy got to her feet and opened it. To see Isabella Arcachon standing there waving her arms around as if she was a madwoman. With an expression that exactly mirrored Caroline's.

'You saw her then Miss Westbrooke?' said the Countess in a shaken voice as she entered.

'I did', came the very nervy reply from the bed.

Mrs Ferrars now took firm command of the situation, promptly shutting the door and locking it.

'Saw what pray?', she enquired, turning from one anxious face to the other.

'The angel of death', answered Caroline, literally shaking from fear, getting to her feet and then clinging tightly onto Lucy's arm for comfort.

'Are not angels of the male sex?'

'This one was not Mrs Ferrars', responded Isabella 'and Miss Westbrooke's description of that ghastly image is no exaggeration. We both saw it. That is I presume we saw the same. I observed quite a young woman wearing a red gown worked with gold and silver and with wild black hair about her shoulders. A face such as you have never seen. It stared at me. Such a look as I never hope to see again either. Purest hatred. A white face. The eyes of the most vivid green. They spoke death.'

'Yes that is what I saw also', added Caroline. 'It is most fortunate that you were asleep.'

'Fortunate, I dare say, for your strange visitor', replied Lucy coolly. 'Were you then awakened by her?', Mrs Ferrars asked of Isabella.

'Yes. At least I woke to a cry which seemed to come from your rooms. I dozed just a little I fancy and then there she was. Standing at the end of my bed. I could not move. Then she walked away.'

'Indeed? In which direction?'

'Why through the doorway', replied Isabella.

'The door which leads to the passageway I presume? Which was open? By which you then walked across to my room?'

Isabella nodded in turn to all these questions

'How long after this apparition had left did you wait?'

'Oh no more than a few moments .Half a minute at the very most. Just long enough to get out of bed and throw on a cloak. In truth I was fearful for the two of you. Also three heads, and pairs of hands, are of more value than one I think, even with a ghost?'

Lucy raised her eyebrows. 'Your fortitude indeed does you credit. Now the passageway is at least twenty paces from your room at one end to our quarters at the other.What is more to reach the stairs at this end one must also pass my door which has remained locked. You said that you awoke to a cry?'

'Yes.'

'That would be my scream', intervened Caroline a bit shamefaced.

'And most understandable it was', continued Lucy with a challenging look at Isabella, daring her now to question that emotion. However, since Isabella's expression did nothing of the sort Mrs Ferrars continued in her analysis.

'Well as the passage provides the only way between the rooms it would appear that the creature must have passed through the locked door of my own room. Though, I grant, ghosts are not perhaps subjects to ordinary behaviour. But if the stairs was also descended then I fancy you must have seen her countess? For from the passageway there is a clear view down to the floor below and, if my memory serves me right there are some forty steps.'

Miss Caroline Westbrooke shook her head. 'She could have run down. There would have been time from the countess putting on her cloak. Anyway ghosts make no sound unless they wish to.'

Isabella nodded vigorously in assent. 'Exactly so. It was a warning. You must both return to Bath.'

'Any such decision shall not be mine to make', replied Lucy looking across to Caroline.

'Then we remain. Perhaps there is a natural explanation after all. Moreover there are other matters to consider are there not?'

'Quite so. I have never heard of a ghost that writes messages. Nor one that leaves presents of hands and skulls neither.Had my friend's nature not been so resolute as I judged it to be you would have been left to handle such perils alone Countess Arcachon.

As it is however I am pleased that we shall continue our stay hereabouts.But there is something you have not told us.

Something more about this ghost, or the skull perhaps, which is the true reason for your fear?'

Isabella nodded and beckoned to Caroline and Lucy to follow her into her bedroom, promptly dismissing two of the maids alarmed by the confusion.

'I should have made mention of it before,said the countess with a set expression. 'Before his marriage to me Philippe was promised to one Suzanne de Poitiers.She was guillotined in the year 1796. The girl was but sixteen.'

'And the remainder of the family?'

'Her younger sister escaped I believe Mrs Ferrars. The others I think were killed.'

'And the sister's name? Could it, I wonder, have been Catherine?'

'Yes I believe.....good god! Your pardon. But how do you know that?'

'I try always to think before I speak or act', replied Lucy, 'but I must be allowed my own secrets.I have little by way of imagination, but Miss Westbrooke being thankfully supplied with that quality we are well balanced. Even, I dare say, as to finding whether a ghost be true or false. History in France, of late though, is real enough. But what has it all to do with your own terror?'

'I will tell you', said Isabella. 'Some months ago my husband showed me a painting.

'A miniature of his former love. The gown she wore was the very same we saw today. Gold and silver on red and with a distinctive lace border of wild roses. Do I lie Miss Westbrooke in stating that it was such a border upon that you saw tonight?'

'You do not.'

'Thank you. However if either of you have further doubts they may easily be resolved. The miniature is now in my possession.'

When Countess Isabella Arcachon had fetched the small painting and handed it to Caroline for inspection, Miss Westbrooke slowly raised her head to look at Lucy.

'There is no doubt of it',she proclaimed, 'the woman I saw and this miniature are one and the same.'

CHAPTER SEVEN

'SUDDEN CHANGES'

After Mrs Ferrars had taken a look also at the miniature of Suzanne de Poitiers a still nervous Miss Westbrooke passed what little remained of the night in Lucy's room while Isabella was equally set upon remaining in her own quarters. Nonetheless the following morning Caroline, in spite of her unearthly experience, turned thoughts whilst busy at her dressing table towards some human concerns which seemed to have been somewhat sidelined.

'Poor Charlotte. Whatever can have happened to her? Oh Lucy. First Rebecca and now her. When too, one remembers your own misfortunes any, it would seem, who are friends of mine are threatened. Have you forgot also Miss De Traile?'

'I certainly have not. 'Catherine must be warned' the message said did it not?'

For once Caroline looked a little angrily at her friend.

'No. I shall not believe it. The thought is unworthy of you.'

Lucy laughed.

'There are many who consider that no action, however dreadful, is unworthy of me.

A little unfairly, for, to the best of my belief, I have robbed no mail coaches, murdered no people in their beds or put babies on the streets to starve. Well it is of no consequence as I care nothing for their opinions. However, since yours is the only one I do much value, I am determined if I can to retain it. Miss De Traile, 'Catherine', may as easy be a force for good as evil in this whole affair and so the message, should it refer to her at all, may be a warning for her safety. You have too hard a notion of me dearest.'

Lucy stared straight ahead with such a fixed look upon her

that Caroline was doubly startled. Doubly, because never had Mrs Ferrars used such an affectionate word to her before, even if, upon a good many occasions, the strong bond term had been passed the other way. It was, in short, so extraordinarily out of character that it could mean only one of two things. Either Lucy Ferrars was practising a deception of feeling at this stressful time or the exact opposite.

Miss Westbrooke had such total faith in her friend that the former option was instantly dismissed. Former acquaintances of Miss Lucy Steele would have considered that a catastrophic error of judgement of course. But in this instance they would have been wrong and Caroline wasted little time on restrained responses.

'I shall never have anything in my heart but love for you Lucy', Miss Westbrooke replied hugging her close, 'and if the whole world judged you guilty I would shout it down. I do not want to hear one word now', she added softly putting her fingers to Mrs Ferrars' lips, 'about past supposed mischiefs. I should always take your part anyway so what would be the purpose in it? I accept your reproof. But it merely confirms, as does your deep regard for me, what I have always maintained. That you have a far better nature than many suppose. And let that be an end of it.'

'Well', said Lucy, with a smile and a shake of the head, 'if I may be permitted to speak upon another matter it is time now anyway, I fancy, for some breakfast', and Miss Westbrooke being in full agreement with that proposal, the two ladies promptly got up and walked to the door.

'Why did they make this passageway so narrow?' complained Caroline as she followed Lucy to the stairs. 'It is not so very hard in our own gowns I grant to keep them from dirt or damage upon these walls.

But just fancy in the days of wider skirts it would have been a most desperate squeeze. I have not the slightest doubt', she concluded emphatically as finally the two ladies stood side by side at the top of the stairs, 'that the whole thing was designed by men entirely for their own uses without even a thought for their wives or daughters!'

Together in this fashion they now began to descend the amply wide stairway. After a couple of steps Miss Westbrooke slipped her arm through Mrs Ferrars' and Lucy turned toward her thoughtfully.

'Yes I am sure that is so. You have a good knowledge of history. When would you say that passage was built? For it looks to me to be before the Civil War.'

Caroline nodded and pursed her lips. 'I think at the time of Queen Elizabeth. Or perhaps the first King James. That is why I am so puzzled by it. For the skirts were so very wide then. I cannot believe I am the only woman to think it a little curious. Though perhaps it is just my fancy.'

Lucy held her gaze as they went down step by step and finally replied as the last one was reached, 'You are not alone in that thought. Though, without your keen wits, I should not have come so quick to it.'

As they took their tea and toast both guests were surprised to see the change in Isabella Arcachon when their hostess walked in to join them. Gone now was the melancholia of the previous evening. Indeed her manner was almost jaunty.

'I have had all the doors to the outside locked and bolted', the mistress of Dufton Park confidently declared. 'There is little to fear. The day is here.'

'Aye Caesar. But not gone', muttered Caroline Westbrooke.

The reference, from Shakespeare's 'Julius Caesar', escaped Lucy. But not its meaning and she nodded thoughtfully as Isabella walked across quickly to the window. After some moments Countess Arcachon spun round and proclaimed in a commanding tone of voice...

'I am afraid though ladies that you must now be confined to your rooms.'

'And if we refuse?' asked Caroline, giving her a very searching look.

Isabella clapped her hands and into the room came three young men all with a certain look and air about them.

'I hope that you will not Miss Westbrooke. The choice is yours. You may go quietly and with a ladylike dignity or be roughly handled. I have ordered cold meats, bread, fruit and wine taken up to Mrs Ferrars' room where you will both remain until the afternoon. At a time of my choosing you will then be released and my carriage will then be at your disposal to return to York. So what is your answer?'

Caroline looked at the men. Who, in their turn, happily let their eyes wander all over her. Hoping of course that she would put up even the slightest objection to going quietly and so need to be, quite literally, manhandled.

'It seems we have little choice', replied Miss Westbrooke after exchanging a quick glance with Lucy. She moved to the door and with a very uncharacteristically aloof expression towards servants, swept imperiously past with an equally frosty faced Mrs Ferrars in tow.

'So we are prisoners' said Lucy when the two of them a little later were sitting on Caroline's bed and locked up. 'Well at least we have each other for company.'

'And for protection.'

Lucy shook her head. 'I think, as I am sure do you, that the countess received a message at that window. But I do not fancy ourselves to be in danger. We are presumed safe under her roof.'

'Little comfort if we are murdered upon such a false hope.'

'I doubt that. If we are trapped it can only be either that Isabella Arcachon fears for our safety or that she wishes, for the present, to keep us from returning to York.'

Caroline was now surprised to see her friend begin to methodically inspect firstly the fireplace and then the tallboy before turning her attention, with still greater concentration, to a small table in the far corner.

Intrigued despite her worries, Miss Westbrooke moved across and saw Lucy staring intently down at the newspaper. It was an old one, dated the 28 of July, which had featured an account of a naval action off Finisterre between British vessels under the command of Admiral Calder and those of the french under Villeneuve. Caroline now bent over the table also to inspect it.

'I had not noticed that newspaper before' , she said with an enquiring upward look. 'Am I so very unobservant?'

'We both know that you are not. It was evidently placed here after we walked downstairs to take our breakfast. But why I wonder?'

'It is not any newspaper. Have you not seen what is written here?'

Lucy took a look at the brief passage to which Miss Westbrooke pointed. The description of her own release from prison and the circumstances surrounding it.

'Well done indeed Caroline.That had quite escaped my notice I must confess. Now turn your thoughts to this if you would be so good. I wonder who Countess Isabella Arcachon saw at that window? Might not that be Miss Cantlemere?'

'Yes I suppose so. Yet she knows nothing of our mission here I think.'

'Perhaps you are right. But even if that is so others may not know that. Consider. She is seen to travel to York. In our company. Then to stay here at Dufton Park.'

Miss Westbrooke nodded with some vigour. ' True. Also I do fear that Charlotte has an unfortunate ability both to do the unexpected and also to speak unwisely, either of which can make one enemies.

'But did you not consider it strange, even so, that she should seem most set against accepting Isabella Arcachon's invitation to stay here and then, just as quickly, change her mind? Then to disappear in such a fashion. If you are correct and that was her at the window I am not so sure her behaviour is not as remarkable as that of the ghost I saw.'

Mrs Ferrars stared hard at the floor and then slowly, very slowly, raised her head.

'It is indeed', she replied.

CHAPTER EIGHT

'IF LUCY'S ONE IS LUCIE T'OTHER?'

True to her word, at just after three o clock, Countess Isabella Arcachon instructed one of the servants to unlock the door of Lucy's room and another one to summon the carriage. Only when the two escapees were safely deposited at Grant House and after they had greeted a relieved Lord and Lady Lunsford, did they prepare to consider the day's events more dispassionately.Lady Anne however, drawing them a little aside from her husband, quickly put a stop to all that by giving them three quite distinct, but equally interesting, items of news.

'Miss Cantlemere has been found. That is the best of it. She is a little weak, but will soon recover I believe. Her aunt attends her.'

'Where was she found Lady Lunsford?' enquired Lucy.

'We are friends. So do please call me Anne as you used to. As I shall presume to call you Lucy and Caroline when we are in private. Unless you would forbid it?'

'I should not have contemplated such a presumption', responded Lucy Ferrars, 'but thank you. I am most happy to agree and can also speak for you Caroline I think?'

'Of course you can' said Miss Westbrooke. 'So where was Charlotte discovered Anne?'

'Upon the steps of her aunt's house. I do believe that she had been bound and gagged.'

'But you made mention', interposed Mrs Ferrars 'that Miss Cantlemere's shall we say 'return' was the best of it. There is darker news then?'

'Yes indeed. There has been an attack. By highwaymen it is thought. Upon a carriage. Only ten miles from York. So they were indeed most bold. And a death. The poor gentleman was travelling with his family here from Bath it seems. It was his own coach too.'

'And his name was Duke Robert Lavalle?', offered Lucy gently.

'I am glad to be your friend. For I cannot but be amazed at your powers. That is the man certainly. The family at least are safe though and have taken rooms at the 'York Tavern'. The Duchess and her daughter, Mademoiselle Lucie, were visited by your father Caroline and also by Lord Minto. Just before they left for London.'

'My father has gone to London?', exclaimed Miss Westbrooke, holding back most of her her frustration and anger for Anne's sake. 'Without even a word to me? I do understand that he was probably unaware of any danger I might be in and that he knows I was in Lucy's company.Yet still, to treat his own daughter so? Well I do think I have some grounds for annoyance?'

'Certainly', said Lucy with obvious sincerity and Anne Lunsford concurred with an emphatic double nod of the head, before Mrs Ferrars turned to look at her.

'At what hour did Lord Minto and the Viscount depart Anne?'

'Oh now let me see. At about two I think. Perhaps just a little after.'

'But before three?'

'Yes. Now was there, pray forgive me, anything else? For I am tired and would rest before dinner. We eat at eight. Unless you would prefer a little later?'

'We are the ones who should ask forgiveness' said Caroline with a tender smile as Anne made her way to the door and Lucy opened it for her, 'and eight is perfectly acceptable for us.'

That time being, as yet, two hours away, Anne Lunsford's guests were shown up to their rooms and, in that allocated to Lucy Ferrars, began finally to ponder all that they had seen, heard and experienced. It was Lucy who opened proceedings.

'So. At an assembly in Bath a note is found. Apparently by Miss Lavalle. That is the reason we are here and we must remember that. For it is the key I fancy to all that has, or will, follow.You agree?'

'Of course.'

'Very well. Now we cannot say who are those hounds it mentions. We may either presume too much upon our reputation to suppose them to be ourselves or too little on it as to deny the notion.What does happen, and it must be meant to, is that we are no longer in Bath, but here in York. Where we have, at least to begin on, the company of your father and Lord Minto. There is also Miss Cantlemere. She is known to be your friend and accompanies us to Dufton Park. After meeting with Countess Isabella Arcachon she seems quite firm both in her attachment to you and, at least partly in consequence of it, against a stay in the country. However she soon has a quick change of heart and agrees to do exactly that.The following morning she arrives for her visit to Dufton and, very soon after, disappears.We have read the Countess' observations upon new arrivals in the city, which she has been most keen to give us, and we must next consider not only the disappearance of Miss Charlotte Cantlemere but also, and forgive me my dear Caroline for I know it distresses you to think on it, a hand with rings fixed upon it which we know belong to our friend and helper Miss Rebecca Frobisher. A strange message is also found nearby by a servant, trustworthy it seems and, after we have made english of that, we return to York to accept the kind offer of hospitality by Anne Lunsford and her equally amiable husband. Again though we must return to Dufton to observe a skull, and, for yourself, though not I, the sighting of a ghost. We are locked in our rooms late the next morning and not allowed to return to this fine city and the company of our friends until well into the afternoon. When, to end up, we are informed of the sudden departure of Lord Minto and Viscount Westbrooke, the death shortly afterward of Duke Robert Lavalle, who had warned you before of danger here, the arrival in York of Duchess Lavalle with her daughter Lucie and the 'return' of Miss Cantlemere, bound and gagged, to the care of her aunt. Can you think of aught I has neglected?'

'No that is a most clear painting of it. But if we are here to find what Lord Minto called the Queen Rat amongst any of these who might be suspected? Sweet Anne I totally refuse to contemplate. Which leaves us with Isabella Arcachon and the Duchess and Lucie Lavalle. Well there is also Charlotte I suppose? Yet, though I hesitate in one way to say it, I fancy she has not the wits for the role. A tool, and a forced one at that, is the very worst I can think of there and a victim sits much easier with me. But I have no doubt', Miss Westbrooke ended with a candid look at her companion, 'that you will state my opinion of human nature is higher than your own.'

'Excepting only the merits of a certain Miss Caroline Westbrooke you are perfectly correct with that notion' replied Lucy simply. 'As always you speak wisely and I agree with much of what you say. Indeed as to Anne, as we shall call her, Lunsford, we differ not at all and with regard to Charlotte Cantlemere I am, I dare say, comfortable enough with that wider umbrella. Perhaps elsewhere I merely hold the mirror from a different place.'

'You see more clearly than do I. And quicker.'

Mrs Lucy Ferrars tutted at this.

'Nonsense. We listen and learn from each other. As I said to Countess Arcachon we are well balanced. That is why we are so respected and so feared for what we do.'

'Yes in a way I suppose', replied Miss Westbrooke, 'yet what pattern can be made from no pattern? Each thought, each action, is as capable here of a good notion as a bad one. Save of course the death of our Rebecca and, I must think at present, the treatment of Charlotte.'

'They are sensible thoughts. Exactly as I have come to expect. But if the mirror is moved a little, no pattern does become one. For good. Or for evil. So let us look at the light. Miss Lavalle finds the note, the Countess Isabella keeps us from harm, Miss Cantlemere is found, Miss Lavalle is safe.The dark then? Well Miss Lavalle finds the note, Miss Cantlemere vanishes and is later found bound and gagged, we are locked up and Miss Lavalle's father is killed. Not forgetting of course that bundle. To which no lighter option strikes me. But that leads me to consideration of another possibility.Which is that these events are in conflict. That two forces is working at the same time to produce them. One for good, the other for bad. And so, mixed up, they seem, as you see it flat on, to make no sense.'

'Hmm. Do I not recall', said Caroline a little teasingly, 'that you said it was I with the imagination?'

'Perhaps then I have learned to develop something of the art, alongside my more natural abilities, under the expert instruction of your good self. The difficulty of course', continued Mrs Ferrars 'is in deciding which path to take.For we need firm rocks to tread on.'

'Well we have some.'

'Indeed?'

'Of course', said Miss Westbrooke 'we are forces for good.Yes even you.that was Miss Lucy Steele', she added rather pertly and Mrs Ferrars, to encourage such humours, wrinkled her nose in a pretence of disappointment. 'And there is another matter', added Caroline more thoughtfully.'Your goods and evils do have a link.The same mother to them. Each path begins with Mademoiselle Lucie Lavalle's discovery of that note in her reticule.We must quiz her soon I think. Though gently. For of course she has no father now.'

Mrs Ferrars stared at the far wall. 'Indeed we must quiz her. Observe her well. The same mother. You call her Mademoiselle. I call her Miss. She has.. no father.'

'Liu-seee!', responded Caroline, turning her friend's face to meet her own and accompanying the action with a voice of affectionate irritation as she almost shrieked out this elongation of her friend's name. Can you please explain yourself?!'

Mrs Ferrars smiled indulgently. 'Most willingly. My thoughts fastened again, as so often they do, upon your own remarks. How can we be so certain that the man that was killed is indeed Lucie Lavalle's father? For, if not, what occurred in that carriage and her own presence, unharmed, here in York, may have a very different look to it.'

'And the second thought?'

'Do you remember the exact circumstances of that message?'

'Yes I think so. Mademoiselle Lucie gave it to Lord Minto did she not? As she observed ourselves approaching she had occasion to open her reticule, then closed it and when she opened it again, the note was inside.You were talking to her and looking at her for the whole time.'

'Not quite Caroline. My attention was distracted a little when the Countess Lavalle made her remarks about the Barbazon family. Since you were in conversation with Miss Louisa Blandford, but also momentarily turned away as I recall, that would seem to me to say that, if Lucie Lavalle was speaking the truth ,there are two possibilities.Now we know, from a conversation you had with her, that Miss Blandford has an interest in the theatre and that the note was in reference to one of Shakespeare's plays. So perhaps it was she who wrote it, passing it to Miss Lavalle when it was safe to do so. T'other notion is that Miss Lavalle, for some reason, had it about her person when she entered and placed it in the reticule when we could not observe her. Whichever of these be true this matter would seem to have now an even greater importance to it. In short Miss Lucie Lavalle', concluded Mrs Lucy Ferrars, 'is either a force for a great good or a still greater evil.'

CHAPTER NINE

'FANCY SAUCE AND A HAIR SHIRT'

Grant House was pleasantly situated near to Clifford's Tower and, as the finest house thereabouts, had long been a venue for the very best society. This particular evening proved no exception for, as Lucy and Caroline descended the stairs, they saw, ahead and below them, a myriad of fine colours and costumes. Once upon that level themselves they were greeted with a smile by Lord Frederick Lunsford who promptly and courteously began the round of introductions. Apart from themselves and Anne Lunsford, it emerged that Eleanor and Catherine Stott, their aunt Mrs Charlotte Poyning and her friend Lady Jane Saxby, made up the compliment of the fair sex while Lady Jane's sons, John and William, along with Mr Thomas Fuller and Frederick himself, represented the gentlemen. There would therefore be a dinner party of eleven, more than enough, felt Frederick, for his wife's tentative return to the social scene. As matters turned out however it was to be even smaller than that.

The ladies, all both having paid their mix of congratulations and concerns to Anne and insisted upon her sitting down, were exchanging small talk (chiefly about the weather), as the gentlemen stood a little to the side. Seizing the opportunity to pay a sincerely felt compliment and also to emphasise his social connections Frederick Lunsford now turned to Thomas Fuller.

'There! Did I not tell you what a remarkable beauty is Miss Westbrooke? Have you ever seen her like?'

The words were spoken in a loud enough whisper fully designed for Caroline's ears to pick up, but were, even so, more softly spoken than Thomas Fuller's reply.

'To speak truth Lord Lunsford', he said with great deliberation, slowly looking Caroline Westbrooke up, down and up again as if she was a heifer he was contemplating buying at market, 'I cannot comprehend the general admiration. Her figure is too slender, her face too pale and her hair needs cropping. Such gowns as that are also far too ornate. Such a delicate doll would not last one winter's day in the north. In all', he concluded with a light laugh and lowering his voice to the level of Lord Lunsford's earlier, 'too much fancy sauce and too little good meat to satisfy a man.'

Frederick had no doubts of course that Caroline had overheard these frank remarks and hastened to do far more than distance himself from them.

'You are speaking sir, under my roof, not only of a lady whom I greatly admire, but who is a particular friend of my wife's. She is also a guest in this house. Your jest, for jest it can only be meant to be, is in very poor taste.'

Thomas Fuller gave a slight shrug of the shoulders and dismissive wave with his left hand.

'I apologise for any offence to yourself and Lady Lunsford my lord' he replied. 'But my opinions were honestly expressed. The lady needs improvement. But I am sure she can answer for herself', he added, turning again to look boldly at Miss Caroline Westbrooke, 'for, as is the fashion with many of her sex, she has listened when she should not.'

'I do not care to talk to you sir', said Caroline, with an equally confident composure that took Thomas somewhat by surprise, 'nor do I care in the slightest for your opinions. If you want to consider work upon improvements I suggest beginning, not with my appearance, which is no concern of yours and with which I am perfectly content, but rather with your own manners. If, that is, you can find any.'

Thomas was not at all accustomed to being bested in badinage by ladies and the admiring glances and smiles in Miss Westbrooke's direction from other members of her sex irritated him still more.

Nonetheless it was the men who verbally backed Caroline up.

'Shall you apologise to this lady sir?', said Frederick, now moving to stand next to her.

'He shall Lord Lunsford. Or face me with the consequences of it.'

The hitherto silent John Saxby's words, delivered with some threat and supported both with emphatic nods and an 'aye' from brother William produced, in a sense, the required result for harmony.

'Of course', Thomas responded with a ludicrously exagerrated flourish of a bow to Caroline. 'You are all a little unkind upon me I fear. Indeed I should be most happy to make Miss Westbrooke my wife, for she is not altogether unpleasing. 'But do first', he concluded in a mockingly helpful tone to Caroline, 'have that hair cut. You would look far better without it.'

'Oh on the very day we marry sir', said Caroline with a contemptuous laugh, 'I shall let you perform the task yourself. I can make a shirt out of my loss too can I not? For to be your wife what apparel could possibly be more appropriate?'

'So much for your wit Miss Westbrooke. But I shall remember you said that', replied Thomas Fuller in such a deliberate and menacing tone that Lucy Ferrars shot a deeply searching look at him. Only now it appeared, was he even aware of her presence.

'I shall remove myself from your company Lord Lunsford', continued Thomas , 'and should yourself or any other', he went on looking directly now at John Saxby with a sneer, 'care to take up the matter of Miss Westbrooke further you may, at a time and place of my choosing, do so. I leave you gentlemen to the safety of the ladies. And Mrs Ferrars.'

'Mr Fuller?', shouted Lucy, making him turn around at the door.

'What madam?'

'I shall remember you said that.'

Conversation at dinner as might be expected, began with some difficulty and the main thrust of the early part of it was in preventing Frederick Lunsford and, in particular, John Saxby, from rushing out there and then to challenge Thomas Fuller to a duel. Caroline helped considerably by laughing the whole matter off and this,with an expression of gratitude for his support and an added smile, was just about enough to pacify Frederick. John Saxby however seemed to belong more in spirit to the High Middle Ages than Georgian England and, once his sensitive eyes had gazed upon this fairytale princess, the suit of armour and fine white charger were mentally being made ready to defend her honour.

Miss Westbrooke looked at him and, as he coloured and glanced down avoiding her eyes, she began, very softly and gently, to speak to the young man.

'I really am most grateful to you for your gallantry Mr Saxby. But if you have a real regard for my feelings you must not pursue this.You are a true gentleman sir', added Caroline as she leant across the table with a hissed whisper in his ear. 'No duels though. I insist.'

'I am entirely at your command Miss Westbrooke', said John with only too obvious sincerity.

'The man is evidently either brim full of spite or else a complete lunatic. I could get a hundred men in a minute to say as much', said John's younger brother William draining his glass of claret.

'Well said sir!', declared Frederick Lunsford, his response given yet more heartily on the strength of two amply sized glasses of the same tipple. 'And he is also blind. For how can any man cast eyes on Miss Westbrooke and not consider all that he sees there to be complete perfection. I am afraid she really must accept these honest thoughts of an evening!'

'Perhaps my lord', replied Caroline quietly and blushing a little, 'since you are the husband of one who is a particular friend of mine I should put a lid upon your box of praises now?'

Frederick glanced at his wife, grinned, and, after a good gulp at glass number three of wine, addressed his final thoughts with a sweeping look from face to face around the table.

'The lid will not alter the delights of the box. What say you Mr Saxby? Do I not speak the truth?'

'Ye..ye..yes my lord', said John, now reddening far more than

Caroline had and desperately searching to look into any eyes rather than the pair he really wished to. As luck would have it they ended up on Lucy's and Mrs Ferrars, just for once, was disposed to help a man out of a predicament.

'What is of interest to me Lord Lunsford is why Mr Fuller should so forcefully express such remarks in company. I confess my great surprise that he does not hold the opinion which yourself and many other gentlemen have of Miss Westbrooke. But he must have known that, if his view was a contrary one, it would cause the greatest offence. If he is so honest as all that he can have moved but little in society I think. Is that then the case?'

'Not at all' said Anne Lunsford, 'for he is to be found at every assembly ball and is much desired as a partner.'

'But no longer by me Lady Lunsford. There are other ways of wearing Miss Westbrooke's favours than by duelling.'

Catherine Stott spoke with a gravity belying completely her pretty but somewhat vacant face. It was a curious mixture noted keenly by Lucy Ferrars, as Caroline's warm smile to Catherine for this open support from a member of her own sex expressed her thanks far better than any words could have done.

'I was surprised', said Mrs Jane Saxby, 'that Mr Fuller's sister was not present. Is she indisposed Lady Lunsford?'

'An invitation was sent to her' replied Anne carefully, 'but she has a cold I believe.'

'My daughter also is not well', said Jane quickly, with an uncertain look in Caroline's direction. Noted again of course, as all was noted, by Mrs Lucy Ferrars.

'Well our dinner table certainly might stretch itself to fourteen' responded Lord Frederick Lunsford. 'In point of fact we had sixteen about it when the Duke and Duchess of Devonshire called upon us. What a squeeze that was! Though her ladyship was quite charming I recall and not at all put out. Yet twelve, well ten now I suppose, is a happier mix I fancy.'

'Might I ask Miss Westbrooke, if it is not too great an imposition, that you will pay a call upon us tomorrow afternoon? Or indeed the afternoon following if you prefer that? Mrs Ferrars also if she would be so good.'

'Oh please say you will Miss Westbrooke' said an imploring Catherine Stott after her aunt Mrs Poyning's request. 'I do declare that I shall never make sense out of Mr Fuller's odd remarks.'

'Of course' said Caroline, though whether this was in response to Catherine's plea or the comment that followed it was impossible to say. But, at any event, a visit to Fawkes House, Petergate at three the following afternoon was settled upon.

CHAPTER TEN

'WONDERFUL MISS WESTBROOKE!'

The next day, having passed a most agreeable morning in the company of Lord, Lady and baby Lunsford, Caroline Westbrooke and Lucy Ferrars found themselves, as arranged, at Fawkes House. Lucy was hopeful that, in private, Mrs Charlotte Poynings, aunt you will recall to the two young Stott ladies, would prove to be a chatterbox and she was not to be disappointed. To begin with fashion was the theme and Miss Caroline Westbrooke held court upon the sole topic of conversation for fully half an hour.However, pleasant and diverting though this discussion was, the afternoon was to prove to have rather more to it than that.

'Well Miss Westbrooke. Your reputation has gone before you and I can observe for myself that it is entirely deserved. But must you really capture every man's heart in York as well as in Bath? Shame indeed! For now my poor nieces must wait until your departure before any attentions are paid them.'

Though Charlotte Poynings' voice had a harshness to it the expression on her face did not and so Caroline replied pleasantly enough.

'These ladies will fare very well I am sure whatever is thought of me Mrs Poynings. Moreover, if Mr Fuller's opinion is not unique I shall be somewhat short of admirers in Yorkshire. I quite surrender him.'

To Caroline's surprise this received not, as she had intended, easy laughter, but rather only smiles of sympathy and, in one case, an angry response.

'I quite detest that man and how he could have such sentiments in his head, let alone have the appalling bad manners to express them is beyond me. For my part I love your gowns Miss Westbrooke and

57

now, having seen the arrangement of your hair, am quite determined to grow mine very long also so that, if you will be kind enough to forgive the presumption, I may copy it .Or as near as I am able. For it is quite remarkably lovely. Whatever, also, can you possibly eat to possess such a fine figure? Would you tell me in confidence? You have told us now of all the latest fashions. I do so agree with what you say. But would you advise me? I mean as to my own appearance? What colours would become me? You must pardon me. But I always speak my mind. Is that not so aunt?'

'Yes and I have often urged you not to', replied Charlotte Poynings solemnly. 'Though in this instance', she added with a bright smile for all, 'you are pardoned.'

'And I certainly prefer your opinions Miss Catherine to those of Mr Fuller', added Caroline laughing freely for the first time since the discoveries at Dufton Park and also throwing up her hands in response to the younger Stott sister's flood of praises. 'As to the rest I shall be delighted to talk of clothes.Though judging both by your gown last evening and your appearance today you need no advice at all upon the subject.'

'You have a lady champion too it seems Miss Westbrooke' said Charlotte quietly, noting Catherine's flush of pleasure at the compliment to her favourite, and very carefully chosen, white 'afternoon dress'.

'Yes aunt she has. A friend too. An offer I extend to Mrs Ferrars. For she was also greatly insulted.'

'Thank you Miss Catherine' said Lucy eyeing up the young woman very carefully. 'Then, as our friend, have you aught else to tell?'

'Well Mrs Ferrars the Fullers are a strange family. Thomas, Mr Fuller, I liked well enough. Until yesterday. But odd.'

'Odd?' said Caroline softly. 'I recall you used that term yesterday with regard to him. How pray?'

Catherine coloured a little and looked uncertainly at her sister. 'Well he has said nothing indelicate to me Miss Westbrooke. But you do not have a monopoly on his insults to ladies. I - would not wish to say more.'

58

'My sister is very loyal and also considerate' intervened Eleanor Stott, touching Catherine's hand, 'but I am happy to speak of it. My face has been called too red, my white muslin gowns,of which I do confess I wear many, are too simple and, like yourself Miss Westbrooke, you will have noticed my preference for long hair. Mr Fuller must be somewhat firm, as some gentlemen are I presume, upon that point.'

'Very firm indeed' said Caroline heatedly, 'on a matter which, as I made most clear to him, is none of his business. But I fancy now that we are not your only visitors. There are voices at the door. Mrs Ferrars and I must make our farewells.'

'By no means' said Charlotte Poynings and in a few moments the guests had swelled from two to five.

Once introduced by her eldest brother, Miss Louisa Saxby proved to be a far more talkative and less self conscious member of that family than did he and began a long conversation with her mother and the Misses Stott upon music and dancing, soon seeking also the opinions of Lucy and Mrs Poynings. Which left John Saxby seated opposite to Caroline Westbrooke and in conversational purgatory. Between the heaven of his hopes of getting everything right and the hell of his fears of getting everything wrong.The more he wished to speak the more his courage failed him and so, quite certain after a minute or two that the object of his adoration would consider him either foolish, dull, weak, witless or probably all four, he resolved to avoid any further disasters by studying the far wall. Only then to mentally add incivility to his supposed crimes. Caroline always took very great satisfaction in adding another male admirer to her lengthy list of conquests, but she was also a flirt with a heart, especially for men seemingly not so sure of themselves as she was, and so made it her business to draw John into conversation. In addition too she had not forgotten that support at Grant House and so he stood somewhat higher in her estimation than he imagined.

'I am truly glad to see you again Mr Saxby. Have you been long in York?'

'Ermm..'.some three months Miss Westbrooke. We are staying at our town house. It is but small. I prefer the country, but my brother and especially my sister enjoy company and balls. Indeed we are to hold a small reception, with some dancing, tomorrow evening. We can take but eight or nine couples at most. I am here to ask the Miss Stotts. My brother William would be here also were he not on similar duties elsewhere. I do wish mother would not be quite so hasty in such decisions. Of course it is her way and people in York know that but one cannot expect', he added regretfully with an apologetic glance, 'strangers to agree to it.'

'And have you your complement then? Or could you accomodate two ladies from Bath also? Mrs Ferrars and I would be content to watch', replied Caroline serenely.

John Saxby could hardly believe his ears. Still less his own reply.

'Oh Miss Westbrooke. How very gracious and understanding of you. Mother will be delighted. For she was most insistent that I extended the invitation to yourself and to Mrs Ferrars. Indeed', continued John, lowering his voice, 'I have already paid a call at Grant House. I do beg your pardon for quite forgetting that you were to visit Mrs Poynings and her nieces. I have been unpardonably rude in not requesting your company before any other. But might I request then, if you would be so kind, the first dance?'

Caroline smiled and coquettishly put her head on one side. 'On one condition Mr Saxby.'

John looked back half expecting mockery and half annoyance. He saw neither.

'Of course. Yes. Anything. Thank you Miss Westbrooke.Thank you.'

'You have not heard my terms yet', responded Caroline demurely, playing with her long ringlets and casting her eyes down.

'No. I am sorry. Please forgive my rudeness.'

'You are not rude at all' said his golden haired goddess looking quickly up again. 'But I am new to York. So they are easy terms. To talk, now, entirely to me and devoting yourself to no other for the remainder of the afternoon, of the shops, the theatre, the dances, the people. All that may be done and all who are of consequence. Or even not, if they are amusing or interesting. I am, when I wish to be so, a good listener. Indeed, if you agree to answer all my questions to my satisfaction', she concluded with a sweet smile, 'you may have the last dance also if you wish.'

The best John Saxby could manage to this delightful prospect for the present and future was a nod for each and he knew that to be most ill bred behaviour towards such a high born lady. Nonetheless, by her kindly expression it really did seem that Miss Caroline Westbrooke didn't seem to mind the lack of customary gallantries and, little by little, spurred on both by that look and the encouraging smile that went with it, he warmed to the informative task that she had given him. In two minutes he was a lost man.

Lost in the temple he had built in his head to the worship of wonderful Miss Westbrooke!

CHAPTER ELEVEN

'THE LILY AND THE ROSE'

On entering the elegant residence of the Saxby family close to the river on Micklegate both Lucy and Caroline considered that John had done his home considerable injustice. Modesty was a virtue in general that they considered rather overrated, but there were exceptions, especially in gentlemen, so that the smiles given to the elder Saxby brother had no artifice in them.

Very soon the assembly either took to the floor for the opening dance or a chair from which to observe it. There were eight couples. Who faced up to each other as follows.

Mr John Saxby.	Miss Caroline Westbrooke.
Mr William Saxby.	Mademoiselle Catherine Barbazon.
Sir William Matthews.	Miss Belinda Fuller.
Lord Frederick Lunsford.	Miss Louisa Saxby.
Count Philippe Arcachon.	Countess Isabella Arcachon.
Mr Martin Andrews.	Miss Catherine Stott.
Lord James Saxby.	Miss Charlotte Cantlemere.
Sir Charles Denton.	Mademoiselle Lucie Lavalle.

Joining Lucy in observation were, seated at opposite ends, Countesses Barbazon and Lavalle talking to, respectively Mrs Andrews, Charlotte Cantlemere's aunt and chaperone and Mrs Poynings, fulfilling the same duel role for Catherine Stott. Lady Jane Saxby meantime moved from group to group as hostess.This leaves us only Anne Lunsford and Eleanor Stott to mention for completion of the party and to whom Mrs Ferrars quickly became engaged in conversation, they being seated, respectively,on neighbouring seats to her left and right.

'Do you not consider it strange and most improper?' ventured Anne, 'that Miss Fuller has no companion?'

'We live in strange times', replied Lucy 'and I dare say Mr Thomas Fuller would hardly find a pleasant reception here. Yet it does give me thought when you mention it. Should she be seeking attention and comment she will surely achieve it.'

'Not from Mr Saxby. His eyes have never left Miss Westbrooke. Yet she has a rival this evening. For his brother seems equally devoted to Mademoiselle Barbazon since she arrived yesterday from Bath. I understand it was only his pleading that made her agree to be present.'

'You will forgive me Lady Lunsford', said Eleanor Stott, 'but Miss Westbrooke has no rival this evening.'

Both Anne and Lucy nodded and smiled to Eleanor without replying. As the couples danced on,skilled step matching skilled step, Mrs Ferrars admitted to herself that Miss Stott was wrong. It was a unique experience for both Caroline and her french rival to see their hitherto invincible feminine force fought to a stalemate, but there it was and, for the two Saxby brothers, it was equally inevitable that two dances were claimed with the other's opening partner. Caroline and Catherine were also alike in recognising and appreciating the desire of every gentleman present to achieve excellence when paired with them. Both were superb dancers, but, with encouraging smiles and subtle helpful hints to the men and models to copy for the women, the whole assembly had a far greater proficiency by the time the final bows and curtseys had been exchanged.

John Saxby then escorted Caroline to a corner seat and proceeded to sit down next to her. Miss Westbrooke looked searchingly at him. For a few moments they were alone and, for rather different reasons, both wished to take advantage of it. Guessing what might occur it was the lady who seized the initiative.

'Are the winters cold in the north Mr Saxby?'

John was a little puzzled. 'Sometimes Miss Westbrooke.'

'I see. And you keep good fires?'

'Yes indeed.'

Carefully rearranging little folds in her skirts, Caroline turned a searchingly sympathetic look his way.

'It is not always wise', she began, 'to stand too close to a fire. It means you no harm of course. But if you are burned that is little comfort. And, if you take my meaning, you are too nice to burn. I would prevent that if I can.'

John held her gaze this time as he whispered a reply into her left ear. 'Thank you for your delicacy. However such nobility of character and tenderness of feeling merely increases my fascination for the flames. And I would rather be roasted over and over on your spit than freeze.'

'Then you are set upon martyrdom sir. There is little I can do.'

'We shall see as to that, bewitchingly sweet and beautiful enchantress. For I am quite resolved to win you.'

This was a far bolder John Saxby than Caroline had met to date and she was almost, though given the first part of the declaration not quite, regretting being so considerate. The arrival on the scene of Lady Anne Lunsford however prevented any response.

'Really my dear Miss Westbrooke', said Anne, with firstly a smile to her as she approached the seats and then an amused sweeping glance at not only John Saxby but also Mr Martin Andrews, Sir William Matthews and even her own husband who were all fixedly gazing in the same direction, 'we ladies shall simply have to lock you up! But that too is impossible I suppose. For what gentleman would never speak to us again if we did?'

'Mr Fuller would' said Caroline, with a candid look at his sister Belinda standing a little aside from this impressive gathering which included also Lucy Ferrars, Charlotte Cantlemere and the two Stott sisters.

'Oh do not concern yourself with him, he has always been a tease' replied Anne Lunsford with a smile. 'Once, when I was fifteen, he put two snails on my best white muslin. I screamed for I was sure it was quite ruined. So he laughed, called me a silly goose and said the snails moved faster than my wits.'

'To have a fine gown, especially a white one, stained, is no cause at all for humour and I do not wonder at your response' said Caroline.

'My brother does not hate you either Lady Lunsford. As he does Miss Westbrooke.'

Startled all bystanders turned to look at the speaker. Belinda Fuller, having the floor to herself, continued talking.

'I came here without company as you all will have noticed.That is because I wished to say that I have no desire to be thought the enemy of anyone here. I have spoken only to you what I said to my own brother. But Thomas, that is Mr Fuller, is different. So I come to warn you Miss Westbrooke. He often now boasts in our house that he will marry you. That 'she' has promised it. That 'she' will deliver you into his hands. Of other things too. That 'she' will have great power after the invasion. My brother is but a tool I think. If 'she' is here tonight', added Belinda angrily looking from female face to female face, excepting only Lucy and Caroline's, 'then I say to her that I shall not help in any designs. I want no part of them. I shall leave now and alone. For I came on my feet and, so, shall travel back by the same means.'

'Come' said Caroline gently 'and sit by me as a friend. You shall not walk home. I will not hear of such a thing.'

'No indeed' added Anne Lunsford. 'You may return in our carriage Miss Fuller.'

'You are quite forbidden to walk', said Frederick Lunsford seriously and a little sternly and Lord James Saxby also nodded.

Belinda looked suspiciously all about her. But seeing only concerned and, at worst, neutral expressions, she cautiously sat down next to Caroline.

'My brother cannot understand why I have a regard for you Miss Westbrooke' said Belinda carefully and a little diffidently. 'But I have never had a jealous mind toward those more favoured by nature or circumstance than myself unless they give me cause. You are very kind to offer the hand of friendship considering my brother's grossly improper behaviour. My mother laughed when he told us of it. I did not.'

'Thank you', replied Caroline, pleased, but just a little taken aback at the freedom of this conversation. 'I shall I hope, continue to be worthy of your esteem.'

Belinda looked her straight in the eye.

'I have no doubts at all of that. You have a good friend in Mrs Ferrars too.'

'She has' said Lucy giving Belinda a very searching look as Miss Fuller continued looking at Caroline. 'So have you something then to tell me?'

'Something I found rather', said Belinda hesitantly, turning about. 'In my brother's room. The reason I am here alone. For my mother refused to accompany me. I had to come. Every word I said to and about Miss Westbrooke I would repeat to any. But there was more than just a friendship to give.'

Lucy nodded. 'I guessed as much.'

Miss Belinda Fuller now got up and, as she did so, pressed a piece of paper into Lucy's hand. Mrs Ferrars, by now of course, was hardly expecting anything else as a gift. In an instant it found its way from hands to reticule. Inspection of its contents could wait and, taking advantage of an increasingly heated discussion on the far side of the room, Lucy suggested to Anne and Caroline that they join it. In spite of Miss Westbrooke's entreaties that Miss Fuller should accompany them, Belinda was now set upon leaving and so a carriage was duly called for.However this took some moments and, since Caroline at first insisted upon sitting with the young lady until it arrived and then walking with her to the door when it did, Miss Westbrooke missed the argument. Which was a pity in a way. Since she was partly the subject of it.

'If Bonaparte's army crosses La Manche - the 'Channel', all that are french will be made to come from their holes. Then we shall see who are the rabbits and who the snakes. I say this in english mademoiselle. So all may understand it. The servants too if they can hear me.'

'Since you are shouting now I think that they will Mademoiselle Lavalle' said Catherine Barbazon smoothly in answer to this statement. 'You consider myself and my family to be snakes?'

'I do.'

'And Les Lavalles? They are strange rabbits indeed who take Bonaparte's gold to hide from him in England.

'You lie Mademoiselle Barbazon. But do tell me', continued Lucie Lavalle with a pointed look from Catherine across to Caroline (who was just getting up from her chair to walk with Belinda to the waiting coach), 'how does it feel to be only the second most admired lady this evening?'

Catherine Barbazon laughed. 'I do not consider any here my better. Many englishmen prefer a french lily to an english rose. And among frenchmen', she concluded with an air of considerable satisfaction, 'the lily often has an advantage I think.'

'Do you consider mademoiselle' said John Saxby, 'that frenchmen will also soon be in England to prove the truth of your words? Or rather, when they behold Miss Westbrooke, to give the lie to them?'

'Not at all' replied Catherine with an easy smile, adding 'and I did say 'often' sir. A truly lovely rose', she added looking very steadily at Caroline as she now walked towards the group, 'is as fine an ornament as might be wanted in any country's garden.'

Thanks therefore to the studied good manners of Catherine Barbazon the tensions which Lucie Lavalle had set in motion were smoothed away. Only to be replaced by others as the guests assembled for departure. A tabby cat had been patrolling around the entrance doorway and had instinctively followed its new friend Miss Westbrooke, (for Caroline adored cats), into the room. But before the animal could get further than jumping onto the chair beside which Count and Countess Arcachon were standing, Marie Barbazon, with a loud cry, pushed her way through and shooed it out by the route it had come. Having done so she turned instantly to Caroline, the chief victim of her shoving.

'My pardon Mademoiselle Waystbrook. Mais les chats..oh non.'

'I understand', answered Caroline completely insincerely, carefully examining her dress and most relieved to find it not torn by the encounter. She was uncertain what to add, but Isabella Arcachon saved her the trouble.

'You dance delightfully Miss Westbrooke. You also Mademoiselle Barbazon. Yet some balls are best forgotten even so for others. Especially when one sits? Is that not so Mrs Ferrars?'

'Perhaps' said Philippe Arcachon, 'Mrs Ferrars found other matters of interest?'

'I find much of interest in York at present Count' replied Lucy.

'It is not always wise' said Philippe, 'unless one is at the card table, to return home after an evening with more than one began with. Do not gamble heavily Mrs Ferrars', he concluded. 'The stakes are often too high.'

'Not if she wins Monsieur le Comte.'

Catherine Barbazon's quiet reply took everyone, even Lucy, by surprise and not until Caroline and Mrs Ferrars were in their rooms alone later was mention made by Miss Westbrooke of it.

'It was an interesting remark' said Lucy. 'As was those of Mademoiselle Lucie Lavalle and Miss Fuller earlier. But not so interesting I fancy as made to us by your friend Miss Cantlemere.'

'Charlotte? But she said nothing to me. Everyone else spoke. Even Miss Catherine Stott, though we had little time together. But from Charlotte not a word. Though she must have listened well enough.'

'Exactly', said Lucy 'that is what I meant.'

CHAPTER TWELVE

'THE WOMAN AT CASTLEGATE POSTERN'

'They know the great whore', said Caroline after she had made the translation of the note given them by Belinda.

Lucy shook her head.

'Pray forgive my mentioning it. But there is a stop after the first two words.'

Miss Westbrooke shrugged her shoulders dismissively as she played with her string of pearls. 'So. What of it?'

Lucy became a touch exasperated. Right now she needed the rational sensible Caroline not the fashion conscious vain one. However, as so often, they were inextricably mixed up.

'They know. That is one remark. The Great Whore is another. Your pearls are truly splendid but..', concluded Mrs Ferrars with a sigh and as sweet a smile as she could muster.

'I am sorry Lucy' said Miss Westbrooke with one last touch at the pearls before putting her hands on her lap. 'Really I was listening. But can one make so very much from it? What do you make from 'The Great Whore' that I do not?'

'Well I dare say if 'they' know it might mean an alteration in plans?'

'Ah! You fancy then this 'Great Whore' is, in some way, a clue or guide to follow. Maybe she is the Queen Rat we seek?'

Lucy Ferrars looked thoughtful. 'There may be a more simple answer.'

'What?' replied Caroline a touch petulantly as she now devoted her attentions to the new gold bracelet on her left hand.

'It may come to mean an alteration in the sequence of hidden letters. For future messages.'

'Possibly' said an unconvinced Miss Westbrooke, 'but if it is how are we to discover it this time? If it has been changed for reasons of secrecy the task will be yet harder than before.'

'I am a great believer in time providing answers to difficult questions. However let us turn to another matter of some importance. What are your feelings as to Mr Saxby?'

Caroline looked pert as she picked at the pearls again 'Oh he was not at all helpful. I tried you know, to find out something of value to us We talked first of the theatre and then shops. Like many gentlemen I'm afraid he was of little value upon the first and none at all as to the second. His knowledge of York society also, which was my real purpose in quizzing, was of such a vague character as to make me almost fall asleep! As company though, I found him quite sweet at Fawkes House and, until his too great boldness at his own home, the same there. I shall never marry him of course.'

'Indeed? It seems obvious that he is completely in love with you.'

'Well I know that Lucy! Pray allow me some wits! ' But I am not with him. So where is my gain? I have done my best. Honestly I have. Can I help it if he still wishes to devote his attentions entirely to me? Anyway I have never prevented any gentleman from looking elsewhere if he prefers to. Or objected if he has.'

'Generosity indeed', said Lucy dryly, looking up at the ceiling as Miss Westbrooke put her hands to her mouth and began to giggle, 'yet Mr Saxby's manner to you - setting aside that one instance at the ball - is not at all what Countess Arcachon led us to suppose. I wonder at that.'

'She is married' replied Caroline, keeping a twinkle in her eyes.

Lucy nodded thoughtfully 'She is indeed. I thank you for reminding me of it. What of Miss Fuller now? She seems to have a regard for you much at odds with that brother of hers.'

'Yes', answered Miss Caroline Westbrooke, now becoming intent and serious .'I was most grateful for that. But I worry now for Belinda Fuller. She was very brave to speak out so and surely we must try to help her all we can? Unless you think her false?'

'No I do not. Families, as I know only too well, can go their different ways sometimes - and fall out because of it.'

At that moment Anne Lunsford came in with both a letter and a request to join her downstairs in the drawing room. While Miss Westbrooke was assuring her of their acceptance of the latter in a half hour Mrs Ferrars opened up the correspondence.

'This indeed is from Miss Fuller' she said in response to Caroline's enquiring glance, 'and she requests that we make the short walk from here to the Castlegate Postern at three this afternoon. We Caroline. Not I.'

The weather was not especially pleasant, but thankfully, by the time that the two ladies had set off down the street, their umbrellas were barely needed. They reached the postern at five minutes to the hour, but could see no one answering Belinda's description approaching either from the direction of the city or by way of the road the other way. At ten minutes past they were set to leave when the beggarwoman they had been carefully ignoring and who had been skulking in the gateway came forward to touch at Caroline's arm.

'Spare a coin beautiful lady. A coin for the poor.'

Lucy was about to try to prevent Miss Westbrooke's kind heart, as it usually did, from yielding to this type of plea, when she felt her own hand pressed so tightly that it made her cry out.

'Devil take you then', said the beggar as she ran off through the postern towards what would soon become open country. Mrs Ferrars opened her hand and, placing the next in the seemingly never ending sequence of mysterious written messages into the trusty reticule, she linked her arm with Caroline's and they walked back down Castlegate.The ladies had almost reached Grant House and the prospect of a cup of afternoon tea with Lady Lunsford when, from across the street, they became aware of a crowd of people gathered. Recognising a familiar face now at her side, Caroline asked what had occurred.

'Oh good afternoon Miss Westbrooke. Well I am not quite sure. For I have but just arrived myself . But Bel.. Miss.. oh pray forgive me. It is so dreadful.'

'Take my hand', said Caroline gently but firmly to Miss Catherine Stott. When the girl had done so Lucy released herself from Miss Westbrooke and pushed her way forward. What she saw caused even the normally unflappable Mrs Ferrars to draw in her breath. For there, upon the pavement, with an arm outstretched and her white gown and light blue shawl both liberally spattered with blood, lay the body of Belinda Fuller. Nor did there seem the slightest doubt as to how she had met her sad end as a dagger lay still buried in her heart. Having now seen all that she felt was necessary, Lucy Ferrars returned to the watching Caroline, who was comforting a weeping Catherine Stott. It was to the latter that she spoke.

'I fancy you should accompany us. For there is something to say I think.'

CHAPTER THIRTEEN

'CAROLINE, CLOTHO OF CLOTHES'

'Now Miss Catherine', said Lucy sternly, 'I want the truth. You are 'forgiven' as you wished. But the 'Bel' you so far forgot yourself to speak would have turned into 'Belinda' I dare say. So you were not slightly acquainted at all with Miss Fuller were you?'

Catherine Stott shook her head.

'And her death causes you alarm as well as sadness.I am a good reader of a face and what it expresses. Your friend is dead both because she knew too much and was brave enough to think and speak for herself.So, for your safety and her revenge, pray tell Miss Westbrooke and I what you know of this affair.'

'Very well Mrs Ferrars. I must trust you. Belinda and I have been close acquainted since we were children. As the years passed we grew close and had dreams to be sisters. That was more in Belinda's power than mine and so she made every effort to make me agreeable to her brother as a match.'

'I see. So she was partial for you to marry Mr Thomas Fuller? That is of interest.'

'I quite detest the man.'

'And yet you rather liked him at one time? Before his insults to Miss Westbrooke.'

'In a way only. It was more that he had a power over me. Over women. He always has possessed it. He is most handsome, I cannot deny him that even now and, for me in my circumstances, also a good match. But now I feel nothing but contempt for him.'

'Indeed. Quite. And do you consider' added Mrs Ferrars, 'that Mr Thomas Fuller had a hand in his sister's murder?'

'I should not like it recorded that I said I did not.'

'No. I am little surprised at that. Such is not a wager I would care to place either. Please listen carefully. We shall send you home in Lady Lunsford's carriage as soon as that can be managed. Stay close to your aunt and sister at Fawkes House and never, for any reason, go out alone. If you do as I say there is no need to be frightened. Should Miss Westbrooke or myself need to speak with you again we shall do so at your home.'

'It is now time' said Lucy after a still tearful Catherine Stott had been despatched to her aunt's in Petergate, 'to consider our paper.' Which, when opened out, read thus...

ehhi nmmamm lamm iohmie mln. mmh mimi ahnltham aaemmh. olnn iha ei mhnmmmm mila.

'Your thoughts Caroline? There are, you will note, other letters here.'

'Well in the first place you were obviously correct in the belief that the key to the messages has changed. Also this communication is considerably longer than those others. So evidently the writer of it had a great need to give out more information. Yet it was given to us. By the beggarwoman. What I cannot understand though is why? Surely she would have been better just to write us a simple message if it was her who wrote it? But if not, and she just picked it up, how could she know we would be at the Postern Gate at three?'

Mrs Ferrars nodded. 'Good thoughts.Yet she knew we would be there it seems. Nor do I think she was a beggar.'

'But if she was in disguise then, with Miss Fuller dead, that means..'

'Just so. If the two events join up she is in some way involved in Belinda Fuller's death. Well let us see what we can make of the message.'

After some half an hour of different ideas, none of which worked out at anything like intelligible english, Lucy got up to walk about the room. Only to be stopped by an annoyed Caroline.

'Oh Good God! This bonnet. It simply will not do. The green ribbon is not the same as that upon my new gown and I had so wanted to wear them together. Oh from a distance perhaps, yes, they may look the same. But not to those in good society . It is - ow! Lucy! You are hurting me!'

Miss Westbrooke squealed and laughed as Mrs Ferrars hugged her close.

'You are nothing short of a genius Caroline. For, once again that eye for fashion of yours has unlocked the door to a mystery. On this occasion though you truly are to be admired as it shall put us both upon the road to great wealth.True we have some way to travel yet and no doubt the road will have a twist or turn in it. But we are walking with sure feet and all is owed to that pretty bonnet! Yes I am certain of it.The mystery of 'The Great Whore' is over.'

'My bonnet pretty? Well thank you. But as to the rest I do not understand at all.'

'Yes I am sorry. Pray let me explain. Long messages can be most unfortunate at times. For the more one writes the more may be observed. So it be here. Now. What name do you see?' Hidden? In nmmamm?'

'None I'm afraid.'

'Or here? In aaemmh?'

'No.'

'And now, prompted Lucy, covering over with her two index fingers the last three letters of the first 'word', if so it could be called and the first letter of the second.

'mamm.. emm..emma?'

Mrs Ferrars nodded. 'And here?', she added, covering up likewise the first five letters of the eighth 'word'.

'ham..emma...emma hamilton! Lady Hamilton? The Great Whore?'

'So many in society judged her before Sir William's death', said Lucy nodding, 'for her affair with Admiral Lord Nelson. Yet I fancy much of the resentment was at her low birth and how she had risen so fast in spite of it. From a distance she looks like a lady. But her and good breeding is not a perfect match. Unlike Miss Westbrooke for example.'

'I understand my importance now' said Caroline smiling playfully, 'for am I truly not that Clotho of mythology who began matters by gathering up the wool of life for her friends Lachesis to spin and Atropos to cut? As to Lady Hamilton, though we have never met, I am inclined to like her. She has looks and wits and uses them to advantage. Much like a certain friend of mine!'

'You find no offence in good milk pushing its way up through cream' replied Lucy with a touch of asperity, 'but many 'ladies' are not so generous. Now we must turn our attentions to make some sense out of this last message.'

Caroline, having pulled up a chair, exchanged her stares evenly between her friend's face and the mysterious communication. After a few minutes of study Mrs Ferrars put down her pen and looked searchingly back.

'It would seem now that Lady Hamilton's dangers are much greater than those of simple envy or malice.'

Miss Westbrooke leant forward a little to read out the translation.

'Meet London upon twenty six. One shot delivers France. Kill her at Nelson's ship'. That seems perilous indeed. So we must go to London to save her', continued Caroline glancing up. 'Well I cannot take much satisfaction in my skill. For 'Clotho' stumbled on the right road that is all. But also I cannot see how Emma Hamilton's death can possibly be of any benefit to Bonaparte. Or to the Queen Rat either, who, though a woman and perhaps one of high birth, we must presume to be his instrument.'

'Again, with respect, you forget the stops. Kill her at Nelson's ship is but the third act. To which meet at London is the first. And so?'

Caroline Westbrooke,suddenly wide eyed, put her hand to her mouth.

'Just so' said Lucy Ferrars nodding. 'Lady Hamilton will be but the second course at this blood feast. When one shot will have already delivered up to the Queen Rat, the body of Lord Nelson and with it, most like, England to Napoleon Bonaparte.'

CHAPTER FOURTEEN

'A FAMOUS MEETING'

'But Lucy. You know that I should not at all have objected to lodging with your cousin at Bartlett's Buildings while we are here in London. Indeed I consider Holborn not at all a disagreeable area.'

Mrs Ferrars looked a little severe.

'You may not object Caroline, but I do. However my misgivings are not so much those of social connection - though I dare say I have improved in that regard since our acquaintance begun - but rather of good sense. I am known a little in Holborn and my cousin is not likely to be in greater safety by a renewed meeting. But to other matters. In our time at Brook Street we have discovered that five persons of interest to us have also made the journey from York. Is that not so?'

'Yes. Madame Lavalle and her daughter Lucie, Isabella Arcachon and of course Countess and Mademoiselle Barbazon who were in the same carriage as ourselves. We have little time though to reflect on any of that today. For, do you not recall that we are to meet with Lord Minto and my father. I am becoming impatient. Why are we here? In our time in London we have learned little or nothing and, since Lord Minto seems to have kept his own watch upon Lord Nelson - we saw both of them on the twenty sixth in Piccadilly you remember- and we have also been instructed to keep our distance from Lady Hamilton's house on Clarges Street - our harvests can bear no fruit.'

'I am much of your way of thinking', replied Lucy shrugging her shoulders dismissively, 'but if others watch and wait we must do likewise and hope that all will end well. Lord Nelson and Lady Hamilton are also much at Merton. Perhaps we shall receive an invitation there.'

'Possibly. But what I cannot understand is why no attempt has been made as yet. Lord Nelson especially is seen much about and appears to disregard dangers and I cannot help but think that a little foolhardy. He is no difficult man to trap. We could have set one in the Strand the other day.'

Mrs Lucy Ferrars nodded. 'It is curious I agree. One can only think therefore that a plan has been laid and the time has not come for it. When it does I fancy we shall see our importance. We are to meet though not only with Lord Minto and your father today at Downing Street, but also with Lord Castlereagh the Secretary for War. That I do commend to your notice.'

When Lucy and Caroline arrived they were shown up to a somewhat dull ante room. There was no sign of the Viscount, but Minto was there to greet them and, standing by the window, Lord Nelson himself and a younger man, a little sunburned and with close cropped hair in the uniform of a major general. After the round of bows and curtseys had briefly interrupted their discussion these two began to talk again, or rather, as Mrs Ferrars observed, Nelson talked and his companion listened. Finding after some two minutes, a break in speech, Minto drew Lord Nelson aside and they left the room. The young officer looked for some moments at Caroline Westbrooke before giving her a most courteous and respectful further bow. An intermediary for further introductions not being present the gentleman calmly and confidently strolled across to perform the task himself.

'Miss Westbrooke. Mrs Ferrars', he began turning from one to the other. 'I have the advantage of you, for Lord Minto told of your impending arrival. Permit me then to remedy it. I am Major General Sir Arthur Wellesley. Your servant ladies.'

'Sir Arthur', said Caroline. 'We have heard much of you and of your triumphs in India. Of Argaum, Assaye and Gawilghur. All England speaks your name with pride.'

'All England speaks yours also Miss Westbrooke. I found it hard to believe what I was told, but your beauty truly does outshine even its reputation. For one who has survived a life in tents and a long sea voyage the sight of you is welcome balm indeed. But you praise me a little too greatly I fancy. Especially with mention of Assaye. I lost two horses there, my bay and also 'Diomed' which had been left me by

Colonel Aston. I should not like to see such human losses again either, even in victory, for we had many men killed and wounded. Nonetheless', Arthur Wellesley concluded with a lingering and admiring gaze, 'I am pleased to be held in such esteem by you.'

'Forgive my impertinence Sir Arthur', said Lucy after Caroline had made reply by way of the slightest blush, cocked head and smile, 'for I know little of soldiering. But cannot a battle, indeed a campaign, be performed by patience, caution and stealth? I have read a little of how Bonaparte has won his triumphs. Why I wonder do some always choose to fight such a man in the manner he likes?'

Sir Arthur Wellesley gave a thin smile and grunted a little before giving her a very shrewd and slightly amused stare. 'How I wish I had you on my staff Mrs Ferrars. Should the fates be kind and grant me the opportunity I shall, I promise you, give your notion a good gallop at the french. I have often considered there is more sound sense behind one pretty face under a bonnet than in a whole company of ugly ones under shakos and you have just strengthened the notion. But now I think', he added upon seeing Lord Nelson and Lord Minto returning, 'I sadly must forsake your conversation and that of Miss Westbrooke for rather duller fare.'

'So', said Minto quietly a minute or two later to Caroline after he had seen Lord Horatio Nelson safely inside his carriage , 'you have made acquaintance with Sir Arthur Wellesley? Impressive is he not? His is a star like yours. Destined to shine very brightly I think.'

'And my friend's?' she whispered, looking quizzically from him to Lucy on the far side of the room.

'I was not speaking of you alone', Minto replied.

When Sir Arthur had departed, Lord Minto ushered Caroline and Lucy into their audience. He then closed the door upon them and remained in the anteroom preventing interruptions.

'You may wonder ladies', began Lord Castlereagh, 'why I, and by that I mean the government, have not met with you before?'

'I confess that I did a little my lord' said Caroline, 'but Mrs Ferrars always considered that our time would arrive.'

'Indeed?', responded Castlereagh turning his look and words in Lucy's direction. 'Then it would seem that Sir Arthur Wellesley's high regard for you madam, which he expressed most decidedly to me , is firmly based. Certainly he is', added the Secretary of State for War with a dry chuckle whilst turning from Lucy to Caroline and back again, 'most admiring of you both in many ways it seems. As to your own 'time' it has come now. It is a simple but a critical matter before us and I shall be brief.Today Lord Minto is to dine with Lord Nelson and Lady Hamilton at Merton. At a half after three. Tomorrow evening Lord Nelson departs for Portsmouth to set sail and confront the enemy fleet now assembled at Cadiz. We have the utmost confidence that, from the moment he steps into that carriage for Portsmouth any plot or plan for mischief will fail. So the danger lies at Merton. You two ladies will therefore travel with Lord Minto there where you will remain until after Lord Nelson's departure. As to what best to do thereafter the Prime Minister and myself are happy to leave that to your own good sense. For his part Lord Nelson is aware of your responsibilities and I have assured him also of Lady Hamilton's safety in your hands.The Queen Rat, as we know her, may have more means to give a killing bite. I need hardly say what might occur for instance if her ladyship were to disappear and Lord Nelson learn of such before he sailed?'

'Of course' said Lucy, 'even were she to be found soon after such a delay might prove fatal. Disappear you said. That is curious my lord.'

'It was only one thought Mrs Ferrars.'

'Pray forgive me Lord Castlereagh. My own mind was perhaps, just for a moment, a little elsewhere. Miss Westbrooke and I must make our preparations.'

Castlereagh opened the door and, as his two latest visitors departed, turned to Minto who was standing outside it and whispered dryly.

'Oh the harsh burdens of office my good friend. To have to endure being under the same roof as Miss Caroline Westbrooke, Lady Emma Hamilton and Mrs Lucy Ferrars! How will you survive such a grim ordeal?!'

CHAPTER FIFTEEN

'AS THE FUND OF OUR PLEASURE'

'You play cards do you not Caroline?', said Mrs Ferrars as the two women prepared for their journey to Merton.
'You know I do.'
'Indeed yes. And are most proficient at the art. Speculation. Quadrille. Very accomplished. And at Whist and Loo also you have few rivals.'
'You are my equal at both of those.'
'Whist perhaps. Sometimes. But never Loo. No there Miss Westbrooke reigns supreme. It is a game where success more than usual depends upon the wager one is prepared to place boldly or with caution. So what wager I wonder would you hazard upon our own safety in this enterprise? Considering what we have learned, what we have been told and of the trust we may place in others. Most especially that last.'
'Less than I might wish' replied Caroline solemnly, placing a favourite red and yellow 'spencer' in her trunk and turning next towards her collection of gowns. 'You make mention of cards.Well to determine a value one must count the pips and, if they be a little indistinct mistakes may easily be made and wagers lost. I wonder no one has had the notion of writing a number on corners of the cards. But I beg your pardon. That thought, at present, is of no importance.'
'Possibly not. But it is a sensible one. A lady's notion - and the first such pack to be used should carry your name upon them! Now turn those good wits if you will to three people in this affair, for we yet have a little time before Lord Minto's carriage arrives.Three. Most suitable for the stakes in 'Loo', where of course all must be divisible by that number. I shall charge you, knowing your affection for myself, to consider my life in this and not your own. You have a

stake of twelve. How many would you wager for my life in the care of Lord Castlereagh?'

'No more than three.'

'I see. And Lord Minto?'

'The same. Though I like him well enough.'

'And', concluded Lucy looking very intently, 'of my safety in your father's hands?'

'Three. I would not venture more than that. I do not like to think it, but I must. I answer honestly and would ask you to do the same.'

'Very well. Certainly no more would be hazarded with any of them. Perhaps less. Which means nothing of course. Does that satisfy you?'

'Yes and I am not surprised at it', said Miss Westbrooke, 'for I know your mind as to human nature. So what of me? How much would you stake on your life under my protection?'

'Twelve Caroline. And I would double that if the game allowed. I hope I have the same regard in your eyes?'

'Dearest Lucy of course you have. However, though I resolved never to marry except for love and never to trust any man before that state, I excepted my father. That, even with the strength of our friendship, is a hard thought to put away.'

'Love seems a dangerous game and my advice as to that is to keep your caution in wagers. Though I have yet to sit down at that table. As to your father I do not doubt that he has a love for you such as many daughters never enjoy. But these is indeed very deep waters. Well!' continued Mrs Ferrars more brightly and wishing to cheer up her companion, 'we have yet to finish here. How many gowns do you intend to take?'

'Oh I do not really know. Seven or eight I suppose. But how long are we to remain at Merton? I have my petticoats, shoes, boots - and I cannot possibly manage without my red pelisse and two spencers - oh and my lovely new blue pelisse I simply have to have that - well I may carry it anyway that is something - and yes I need at least these three hatboxes. I can always send back for more of everything if I need to. All these though I must take or I shall be almost threadbare!

Do you not feel the same?'

'Well perhaps' answered Lucy with an amused and indulgent smile at Miss Westbrooke's predictable deliberations, 'my requirements are just a little less than yours! Yet, as you say, we do not know the length of our stay at Merton. I shall content myself though with one pelisse and two hatboxes.'

'How you can bear to? So little?' responded Caroline, genuinely surprised.

Lucy merely smiled and shrugged her shoulders.

'Well if you are quite sure. But there will be space enough in the carriage for more. As for myself clothes are my proudest possession. Well apart from this I suppose', said Caroline laughing and touching at her loose blonde ringlets. 'In truth I would as soon lose my head to the guillotine as my hair to the scissors and I cannot see why that rude Mr Fuller makes such an objection to it. I do not think Mr John Saxby or Sir William Matthews share his opinion though. Indeed much the opposite I fancy! But you need have no cause for envy Lucy. Those curls are quite divine. Somewhat in the manner of Miss Catherine Stott's', she added thoughtfully. 'Though a little longer of course. They suit you very well.'

'What was that you said?'

'Why that you should have no concerns as to your hair. It is..'

'No no' interrupted Lucy, 'before that. You made some mention of the guillotine I think?'

'Only that I would as soon see my hair cut off as my head. A silly thing to say I know. But I do think', concluded Caroline defensively, 'that I have a right to be just a little proud of it.'

Lucy nodded and remained silent for some moments staring at the floor. Before suddenly looking up and replying both brightly and lightly;

'Of course you have and I thank you also for your compliment to mine. Praise from you upon that subject is much to be valued. So. Lord Minto's carriage should be here in five minutes. We have done splendidly I think.That is to say you have. For I but listened.'

'Whatever do you mean?'

'What did the last message say?'

'Kill her at Nelson's ship. One shot delivers France. Meet at London. Oh I have got that - oh I don't know - all gown petticoat and shift!'

'Miss Westbrooke's way of saying three two one for one two three - and most neat done too! But no matter. For I dare say all is to be done with the one shot. Hair as well as head. We have not one murder planned here but two. All is to be cut at once you see. Lord Nelson and Lady Hamilton are to die together.'

'With one shot? Yes I see. 'As the fund of our pleasure let us each pay his shot'.'

'Now your wits are ahead of mine.'

'Forgive me', said the now bonneted Miss Westbrooke peering out of the window and seeing in the distance the approach of a carriage. 'I was merely speaking the words of the dramatist Ben Jonson. A shot may therefore be a reckoning. Money. A stake. Though as to ships?' she posed, taking Lucy's arm as a knock came at the door to announce that trunks, hatboxes and their owners would soon all be on their way to Merton.

'They are not moored inland? If large enough to fight the french? Is that your meaning?'

Caroline nodded in turn to each of Lucy's questions.

'Well perhaps' concluded Mrs Ferrars with a whisper in Miss Westbrooke's ear as the servants now began to take their luggage down the stairs 'ships have more than one meaning also?'

CHAPTER SIXTEEN

'FRIDAY THE THIRTEENTH'

The journey to Merton was made in silence. Lord Minto involved himself in reading the 'Morning Chronicle', while the two ladies observed what they could of the scenery through the carriage windows. At twenty minutes past three they arrived at their destination. But there was no sign either of Lord Horatio Nelson or of Lady Emma Hamilton, who had been a widow now for over two years.

Being soon informed that their hosts had been delayed, Minto passed the time in conversation with two other gentlemen.The name of one meant nothing to him, but the other, a Mr Perry, turned out, strangely enough, to be the editor of that same 'Morning Chronicle'. Lucy and Caroline, being somewhat ungallantly left at a loose end, contented themselves with a walk in the garden until they heard the approaching clatter of horses.

After the initial courtesies had been observed the parties split up by their sex. Lords Nelson and Minto were soon left alone when the other men made their departures, while Lady Hamilton was left to entertain the female visitors.To her relief the mistress of Merton found her guests surprisingly pleasing. Unlike most of the aristocratic females Emma had encountered, Miss Caroline Westbrooke appeared more than willing to be friendly and, as for Mrs Lucy Ferrars, she quickly recognised there another like herself who had risen up through the ranks .Since Emma herself displayed both beauty and a natural charm the potential seemed to exist for a most harmonious afternoon.

But it was evident that, in spite of these virtues,Lady Hamilton was also in low spirits and, at the sight of Nelson returning from his walk with Minto, her conversation dried up completely. With a quick glance and half smile of apology to Caroline, who seemed to her best likely to comprehend and sympathise, Emma then rushed from the room.

'Your pardon ladies', said Admiral Nelson. 'But my impending departure has disturbed Lady Hamilton considerably.If you will be patient I shall do my best to persuade her to return.'

'We quite understand my lord' replied Caroline in such a soft and gentle tone that Nelson looked at her with great suspicion, 'but be assured we are not at all put out. Your absence will be most distressing for Lady Hamilton, but if myself and Mrs Ferrars can assist in easing the situation we shall be most happy to do so.'

All the time that Caroline had been speaking Lord Horatio Nelson had been observing her closely. He liked what he saw and, for once, it was not physical characteristics that had precedence in a man's admiration.

'As I believe you know Miss Westbrooke I leave for Portsmouth tomorrow evening. If yourself and Mrs Ferrars would consent to stay with Lady Hamilton at least until the following morning I should be most grateful. I know from Lord Minto that you have business of your own, but company is important at such times.'

'We should be glad to my lord.'

Emma could not be persuaded to return before dinner and then ate little.The whole mood of the meal was melancholy and it was difficult to know what to say. Talk of fashion and general social chit chat seemed trivial in the extreme under the circumstances, while discussion of the war was also out of the question. Caroline, supported at intervals by Lucy, made some pleasant comments about the garden and, with questions, finally succeeded in diverting Lady Hamilton's mind to this and then to music to such an extent that it earned her yet more praise from their host as he returned from seeing Lord Minto into his carriage to take him back to London.

'Providence has surely sent you here Miss Westbrooke. It is rare indeed for beauty in society to be complemented by a kind heart. You two could I fancy', he concluded looking from Caroline to Emma, 'capture all of Bonaparte's ships between you!'

'You will do that for us my lord' said Caroline with a smile and, after a similar gesture to Emma, and in common with everyone else, she then made her way upstairs to bed.

The next day demonstrated just how much Lady Hamilton meant to England's naval hero as, in front of several witnesses including Lucy and Caroline, Nelson and Emma exchanged wedding rings and took the sacrament together. Miss Westbrooke was in earshot of the couple and, as she later reported to Mrs Ferrars;

'It really was most touching. Lord Nelson took her hand and said ' Emma I have taken the Sacrament with you this day to prove to the world that our friendship is most pure and innocent and of this I call God to witness.'

Now you may well be asking the question as to why Lucy was not there to hear those words clearly for herself. It should be stated at once that it was not because of her social background. Indeed Emma had specifically requested Mrs Ferrars' presence at the forefront of the ceremony. But, upon entering the church, Lucy had noticed standing at the back a woman and determined to position herself opposite her. The stranger was a little above medium height, but most remarkable in that she wore not only a black dress, but also a black veil. At the very moment that the rings were being exchanged this woman walked out. Lucy followed at a discreet distance.

The stranger looked round and, evidently surprised, quickened her step. Mrs Ferrars doing likewise, the woman broke into a run and then, some good way distant, brought, it seemed, from the folds of her gown, a pistol. Which she then fired.

Lucy slowly got up from the path upon which she had thrown herself when the weapon was aimed. There was no sign now of the woman, but the shot had been heard elsewhere and, by the time that Mrs Ferrars had got up, a concerned Emma Hamilton and an almost frantic Caroline Westbrooke lent support to left and right.

'You are unhurt Mrs Ferrars?'

'I am Lady Hamilton thank you', replied Lucy, while Caroline, with a fiercely protective look directed at the outside world, held her firmly around the waist.

'Thank god. Well we must search the grounds. For she cannot be far away I fancy.'

'On the contrary your ladyship' answered Lucy Ferrars, 'if you will but look to your right you will observe a carriage heading out upon the London road at a considerable speed. I should be great surprised were not that our quarry.'

'But why was she here at all?', queried Caroline. 'Surely not to kill you?', she added as Lord Nelson now joined the party.

'Pray tell me my lord', said Lucy to Nelson after giving Miss Westbrooke a little smile and shake of the head, 'was this 'ceremony' with Lady Hamilton publicly known?'

'I am pleased you are unharmed Mrs Ferrars. No. Even Lady Hamilton herself did not know of my intentions.'

'I see. Thank you for your concern my lord. There was no other service then planned by the priest around this hour?'

'None to my knowledge.'

'Then that quite settles the matter. The woman was clearly present to cause mischief. It would appear that her fangs have been, for the present, drawn and yet..'

'Yet Mrs Ferrars?' prompted Emma.

'Aye Caesar. But not gone' muttered Lucy to herself.

'Pardon?'

'Oh. Nothing Lady Hamilton. I was merely reflecting upon an earlier remark of Miss Westbrooke's. Might it be possible to have a word now with the priest? I imagine he is in the church still?'

'If he is not we shall soon find him' said Lord Nelson grimly. But there proved to be no difficulty.

The clergyman was busying himself putting away the communion vessel as the foursome, led by Lady Emma Hamilton, entered the building.

'Mrs Ferrars would have a word with you sir' said Emma.

'One or two little matters only sir. The woman dressed in black standing at the back today. Was she present when you arrived?'

'She was Mrs Ferrars.'

'And was praying?'

'Yes.'

'You have not seen her before?'

'Not that I recollect.'

'Thank you sir. I supposed that would be so. Just one more question if you would be so good. Did you bring the communion wine with you or was it here before you arrived?'

'I brought it with me Mrs Ferrars' replied the clergyman a little puzzled.

'I presumed, again, as much, but had to ask it. That is all I do believe.'

When Lucy and Caroline had returned to their rooms later in the day and were in a position to reflect a little on matters before beginning their preparations for dinner, Miss Westbrooke looked searchingly at her friend.

'You are troubled and not for yourself. But thank goodness you are safe. Oh Lucy if anything had happened. I should have been with you. Well from this moment I shall be. Nor have I forgotten the plot against you. Could it indeed have been yourself that was the intended victim in that message?'

'I fancy not. Though whether my own misfortune is linked to greater ones I am not so quick to dismiss. But what are your thoughts on what has occurred here? I fancy there is little danger from outside these walls for the present. For I see soldiers in the grounds and only a fool would hazard another shot at me today.'

'Well I have much admiration as well as affection for you', answered Caroline, 'and so must be allowed the thought that not only myself recognises your abilities. My own mind can gallop away like a runaway horse, but I do fancy, as you do, that our task will not be, indeed must not be, followed here beyond tomorrow. Lord Nelson departs tonight for Portsmouth to join the fleet. Once he is upon the road there is nothing we may do and I am certain that Lord Minto and Lord Castlereagh have taken every care to ensure safe passage. The Queen Rat, as you say, is no fool and is hardly likely to take a horse back to Merton and shoot us all. Well perhaps she has missed her chance. Though if we are to get our reward she must still be taken. But of what are you thinking?', concluded Miss Westbrooke as she observed the pensive look upon Lucy's face.

'That word Caroline. True we have met with it before. In one of our past adventures. But it disturbs here me for quite another reason. Though I cannot think why.You used it twice.'

'What word?'

'Horse', answered Lucy Ferrars.

In the short time remaining to them before getting ready for dinner the two women passed the time with Ann Radcliffe's novel 'The Mysteries of Udolpho'. Miss Caroline Westbrooke was an excellent reader aloud and, in Mrs Ferrars, had at least an attentive listener. But for Lucy, since the fine writing was lost in the melodrama, the apparent attention was entirely out of politeness to Caroline. After all her friend was only really doing this to calm her after the ordeal earlier in the day. While unnecessary and even somewhat irritating it was kindly meant and she appreciated the thought. However, while sitting patiently and keeping her eyes respectfully fastened upon the reader, her mind turned to more practical concerns.

Why was that woman there? She was waiting, but for what? A chance, a piece of luck? No that was hardly likely. How had she entered? For the gates were shut and Lord Minto's precautions seemed most thorough.

Suddenly there came a knock upon the door. Lucy looked at the clock. It was exactly six in the evening on Friday the thirteenth of September 1805.

'Beg pardon, Miss Westbrooke ma'am, Mrs Ferrars ma'am. But her ladyship asks if you would be so kind as to dine at seven? For the convenience of his lordship.'

'Yes we understand', replied Caroline, and adding, a little to Susan's relief and still more to her admiration, a smile. 'Pray inform Lady Hamilton that we shall be most pleased to do so.'

'Yes ma'am.'

As the two guests walked into the dining room it was evident to both that Emma had been crying. The soup was consumed in silence and Lord Nelson was also most subdued. Both merely picked at their mutton to sympathetic glances from Caroline - who was barely more enthusiastic. All a waste thought the pragmatic Lucy, for it was remarkably tender meat.

Before long it was time for the sweet to be brought in and it was worth waiting for too. Sugar based confections were most popular of course, but this one was as fine a ship of the line as might be imagined and was surrounded by little sponge cakes, one of which was carefully placed in front of each diner.The girl who had brought in the decoration was now joined by three others of the kitchen staff as she began to speak.

'We hope you will forgive our great presumption my lord', the young woman said with a curtsey to Nelson and then Lady Hamilton. 'But we have prepared this gift in your honour.'

'Thank you Sally' replied Nelson, and, as she quickly led out the others after all the curtseys, he put out his hand to pick up the small sponge. Only to feel it, to his amazement, gripped tightly by Mrs Lucy Ferrars.

'Horse! No my lord! You must not eat it! Nor you yours Lady Hamilton. Nor you Miss Westbrooke.'

'Lucy! He has sipped at his Madeira', shrieked Caroline, suddenly grasping was in her friend's mind.

Using both Mrs Ferrars' first name so freely in company and referring to the world's greatest admiral merely as 'he' were indications enough of Miss Caroline Westbrooke's anxiety, but Mrs Ferrars seemed unmoved by it and removed any doubts by taking a good mouthful from her own glass.

'Indeed. Remarkably fine I think.You would much oblige me now my lord', added Lucy to Nelson ,'by summoning the kitchen staff to the hall.'

In five minutes that was done and Lucy wasted no time in getting to the heart of the matter. In the intervening time she had, after first wrapping her hands in two napkins, broken up all the four cakes and put them on a plate.

'A kind thought indeed it was', began Mrs Ferrars as she addressed herself to the servants. 'But a pity that all should not share in it. Certainly those who prepared it. So eat with our blessing.'

All but one took a step or two towards the plate.

'Stop!' shouted Lucy, before turning to the young woman who had brought the sugared ship and its attendant sponges into the dining room.

'Why did you not step forward as the others? I wonder at that. So step forward now and eat the first piece.'

With everyone looking at her the servant made no move. So Mrs Ferrars, after dismissing all the other servants, moved in for the kill.

'You will be the first to eat that cake. For if you will not you will be held and it will be forced down your throat.' In an instant the girl was on her knees.

'Oh please Mrs Ferrars. I did not mean it. I was asked to do it. Please.'

'What is your name?'

'Sally Duncan ma'am.'

'How much were you paid to betray your country Sally Duncan? To take the lives of Lord Nelson , Lady Hamilton, Miss Westbrooke and myself?'

'A hundred pounds.'

'I see. The cake was poisoned by you?'

'No Mrs Ferrars. The little cakes were given to me to place before the guests. I was told by the woman that if I did not...'

'Yes?' said Lucy sternly.

'That..she would see to it that I lost my situation.'

'The woman?' interrupted Caroline in a tone of voice even harder than Lucy's. 'She was dressed in black?'

'Yes Miss Westbrooke.'

'I do not know whether you are a bigger traitor or a bigger fool' concluded Caroline contemptuously brushing away Sally Duncan's plea of an outstretched hand.

'Exactly' said Lucy, adding angrily, 'Lord above, get to your feet girl. What Miss Westbrooke means is do you suppose that, with your task accomplished, with all of us dead, that you would be allowed to live? I fancy you would have breathed just long enough to look at that hundred pounds and never to spend it. Now. Have you been paid for your services?'

'No ma'am. I was to be given the money later.'

'Where? Here at Merton?'

'Yes ma'am. In the garden . By the old wall. At eight.'

'Then you will be there to receive it.'

Waiting at a position where they could see the girl but where she, or any companions she might have, could not see them, required the assistance of Emma and Lord Nelson, but once this was achieved Lucy and Caroline kept watch alone. Under Mrs Ferrars' orders no servants were to leave the building and furthermore both Emma and Lord Nelson were to keep out of sight. The hour came and went and, at a quarter to nine, Lucy instructed Sally Duncan to return.

'It would appear' said Mrs Ferrars 'that you are duped. I confess I am not great surprised.'

'Then I have no reason to keep silence ma'am.'

'You had none before. But tell all you know and Lord Nelson and Lady Hamilton, for your fate must be in their hands not ours, may choose to show mercy.'

'The woman dressed in black. She said only three pieces were to be poisoned. Not four.'

'Indeed? And who, pray, had the untainted one before them?'

'Miss Westbrooke ma'am. The woman said she was not to die. For she had been promised by sea. In marriage to a Mr Fuller. That made no sense until I thought of Lord Nelson and the navy ma'am. So I thought he had arranged it and that Miss Westbrooke was to escape from such a match and was part of the plan. And there is another strange thing ma'am.'

'Yes?'

'That woman, she is no woman Mrs Ferrars. Or if she is why does she wear a gentleman's shoes?'

Lucy nodded. 'I see. Come with me.'

'Yes ma'am. Can I do anything else ma'am?'

'Two things only. Which may be easy done together as I take you to Lady Hamilton and Lord Nelson. Keep silent and pray.'

Lord Horatio Nelson's judgement upon Sally Duncan was more generous than Lucy believed she deserved, the servant being allowed to keep her position. It was also his last action before setting out, at half past ten from Merton, to make his way to join the fleet assembled at Portsmouth. In agreement with his request the two ladies were to remain that evening in any case with Lady Hamilton, but, after her early retirement to bed there was little they could do other than follow her example. However Caroline had one question she wished answering before closing her own eyes.

'You said horse Lucy. Before you stopped Lord Nelson eating the cake. Why?'

Mrs Ferrars smiled. 'As so often it is to you that I must give thanks. For do you not recall your using that word twice earlier and my troubles at it?'

Caroline nodded.

'Well', continued Lucy 'it is this way.It came to me with the cake and with Sally Duncan's remark that they had prepared a gift. All was quiet and calm. Did not you once tell me that the citizens of Troy once brought a wooden horse inside their walls?'

'Yes.'

'And that at night time, when all was quiet and presumed safe, the enemy troops within it opened the gates and the city was destroyed?'

'You recall the tale well.'

'Thank you. It was the same here. For what safer than a little cake to eat? A gift to kill a nation not a city.'

'A country you have helped to save by your sharp wits' said Caroline 'though let us hope' she added more reflectively, 'that the other ending too is different.'

'Indeed? How so?'

'Because' said Miss Westbrooke candidly as she stifled a yawn, 'Odysseus, who made that horse, not only lived to tell the tale, but, of equal importance to us, spent many years wandering free.'

CHAPTER SEVENTEEN

'ALL AT SEA'

'I know what you are thinking Caroline', began Lucy the following morning before they went down to breakfast, 'for, as always, those eyes of yours betray you. It is somewhat strange, is it not, that I should appear more tender hearted than yourself? But, though I do confess I felt different on it yesterday, I fancy that Lord Nelson was right to spare Sally Duncan.'

'Well I do not!' declared Miss Westbrooke passionately, banging her hairbrush on the dressing table. 'She knew full well what she was about and, had she succeeded neither of us would be here now talking about it. I can only suppose that all of Lord Nelson's thoughts were elsewhere. She is a most fortunate servant and has it not occurred to you that she also is free to serve up breakfast?'

Lucy laughed. 'Well that is easy remedied if it worries you. For my own part I dare say I fear no one less than a caught thief, but why not ask Lady Hamilton for the girl to be present to taste all the food and drink?'

'I have more than half a mind to. For I have no intention of emperiling my life a second time -and how could she think that I could betray my country?'

'You were not known to her and so that was not so very great a sin. But what is of interest is what she said of you. Do you recollect it?'

'Of course I do!' answered Miss Westbrooke, taking up her brush again and applying it to her waist length locks with quite unnecessary vigour. 'Yes she certainly cannot know me if she could possibly imagine I would ever contemplate marriage to Mr Thomas Fuller. He is quite the most loathsome, disgusting, insulting and ill bred man it has ever been my misfortune to encounter - and you know you think the same yourself.'

'I have good reason to' said Mrs Ferrars slowly and quietly, 'for, quite apart from his insults and designs upon yourself, I am convinced that it was he that tried to kill me.'

The hairbrush stopped mid stroke. 'Good God! A woman that was no woman? You fancy that was Thomas Fuller?'

'I do. The height was considerable and the aim excellent. I have no doubt that only my throwing myself upon the ground saved me.'

'Then he was the one who gave Sally Duncan the poisoned cakes? Our 'Queen Rat' is a king then?'

Mrs Ferrars shook her head. 'Oh you are right as to the cakes I fancy. But Mr Fuller is not Queen Rat. Remember what Sally Duncan said. About yourself. You were promised by sea in marriage to him? What do you make of that?'

'Nothing. I have never been to sea, nor can I see that any sense may be made out of it. For my father, who must consent to such an arrangement, has not left these shores either. Oh Lucy Lucy', concluded a defiant and suddenly anxious Miss Westbrooke clasping her friend by the hand, 'my father made me a promise that I should never have to marry against my will. I shall not anyway. Even if it meant running away to Russia. You would not desert me though would you?'

'Oh have no cause for alarm on that count Caroline my dear. For without you my power, in every sense, is much lessened. Moreover, though heaven knows many will never choose to believe it, I am also fond of you and would greatly miss your companionship. Doubtless we could make our way in St Petersburg or Moscow if necessary. Yet you see nothing more in the remark?'

It was Caroline's turn now to shake her head.

'Do you not think?' continued Lucy Ferrars 'that 'at sea' is a more likely phrase to use for a promise made upon the ocean?'

'It seems, and pray forgive me' said Caroline gently, 'a small matter when weighed against my happiness.'

'Well take your own words then. I have never been 'to sea'. Nor can 'I see'. May not then 'by sea' refer, not to water or even to sight, but rather be the letter of a name? The letter, indeed, of our Queen Rat?'

'From whom Mr Thomas Fuller takes his orders and by whose command I am promised to him?'

'Just so.'

'But 'C' could be any name. Ah!' declared Miss Westbrooke with considerable satisfaction, 'it may well be Catherine. 'Catherine must be warned' the message said. Or of course' she added more doubtfully, 'Charlotte I suppose. Oh surely Charlotte cannot be the one? Can she Lucy? I know she has little liking for you and I do not understand why. Unless it be that you are known to be my best friend now and not her. But do we not put aside such silliness when we are no longer at school? I cannot think it is Charlotte, but neither can I see Catherine Stott in the part. So it must be Mademoiselle Barbazon. Who is french is she not? Unless there are some I have forgot?'

'You fancy the 'C' refers to a christian name. That is interesting', said Lucy thoughtfully.

'You do not?'

'It was not my first notion. But you are just as like to be right as I. We are to depart from here at what hour?'

'At one this afternoon', said Caroline, as she finished putting up her hair.

'Then let us go to breakfast and lend what comfort we may to Lady Hamilton and think no more for now upon the letter C. When we return to London things may seem a little different.'

Mrs Ferrars could not know just how prophetic those words were to be.

CHAPTER EIGHTEEN
'SHOTS AND SCISSORS'

The carriage journey back to their London rooms had been a pleasant one, made all the more so by an invitation by Lady Emma Hamilton for them to make a return visit to Merton as soon as all the investigations had been completed. Caroline's room was opposite to Lucy's across a narrow corridor and the two ladies had decided to meet in the latter at five o clock.

Lucy took a few moments to settle herself before the looking glass. Once she did so and gazed into it she went very still at what she saw. For the menacing black caped and hooded person she had seen in the church was clearly reflected there, pointing a pistol at her head. Stepping back just a little to close the door, the figure now stood against it.

'Turn around Mrs Ferrars' said a voice instantly recognisable.

Lucy did as she was asked.

'Good day Mr Fuller. You make a poor woman I'm afraid.'

'And you are soon to be a dead one madam.The world will soon forget I think a low born hussy who forgets the obedience due her husband. You have nothing I require. That stupidly vain and foolish Miss Westbrooke of course is quite another matter. She will be joining us shortly. After my companion has completed his work.It will be most interesting to see how impressive she appears in petticoats and with cropped hair. Though the especial pleasure of shaving her head no one shall deny me. That silly fool is your weakness Mrs Ferrars. The little flame of sensibility that warms your cold mansion of a heart. Or am I in error?'

'No. I have always had an admiration and respect for her far exceeding any other of my acquaintance to which, I own, is now added no little affection. Make Miss Westbrooke my weakness if you wish and so make yourself, not her, into the silly fool. I am content with that.'

To Thomas Fuller's increasing irritation neither pistol nor provocation appeared to have much disturbed Lucy's calm manner and so he decided it was time to dispense with preliminaries. Opening the door he waved his hand across the corridor. A few moments later the elegant figure of a smiling Mademoiselle Catherine Barbazon entered. Closing the door she sat down and, fishing in her bag, produced from it a pistol. Which, when pointed, doubled the threat to Lucy Ferrars. Catherine then nodded at Thomas Fuller. Who, with a snide smile, again addressed himself to his intended victim.

'Mrs Ferrars you must now prepare to meet your god. However we shall make this little play last until the end. I congratulate you. You guarded Lord Nelson better than we could have imagined and that whore Emma Hamilton also who some do call 'lady'. My sister, who was so foolish as to break faith, has paid the price and so will you. As to Miss Westbrooke, true daughters of the Revolution cannot wear fine gowns and we shall make a bonfire out of all hers. Pride is a sin and she is brim full of it. In a simple dress however, and with that shaved head, my new wife will begin to learn to know her place and do her duty. Breeding soldiers for the armies of France is a good calling. I am sure that..'

Whatever Mr Thomas Fuller was certain of was not stated as a piercing scream from the adjoining room split the air. Thomas laughed.

'That will be the torn off gown I fancy. And now', he added, grinning broadly, 'for a yet louder wail I think?'

They all listened for some moments. Before the silence again was shattered.

As the pistol shot was heard three pairs of eyes turned themselves towards the door. Fastening there still more intently as steady footsteps approached. The door was opened and Mr Fuller, standing opposite, found a gun pointed directly at his head. Looking beyond and out into the corridor he listened intently for any further sound and, finding none, spoke in an amused tone to the figure now standing calmly before him.

'We took you too lightly it seems Miss Westbrooke.'For I see', continued Thomas, giving Caroline the slow once over as she stood there not only with hair tumbled down and uncut, but also with one shoulder of her gown still on, 'that the job is not even half accomplished. It was bravely done. But have you primed your piece again for me? I doubt it.'

'What makes you think I have but one', answered Caroline. 'Why do you not try to take it from me then and find out?'

'Your wits are very dull', said Thomas Fuller. 'Let me sharpen them. I shall tell you what will happen. I shall kill Mrs Ferrars and then Mademoiselle Barbazon will kill you. Soon that delicate slender arm of yours will tire. Mademoiselle Barbazon and I can wait as long as we wish. Put the weapon down now little doll. The time for playing childish games is over.'

Caroline looked quickly at Catherine Barbazon who had turned her gun now from Lucy to her. Nonetheless she kept calm.

'So. There are three of us. Three chances for a drop of guard. Let us wait and see then.'

One minute became two and then three.

Observing Catherine Barbazon momentarily look towards the wall, Mrs Lucy Ferrars suddenly threw her feet forward and simultaneously pushed with her back hard against the chair. Then, in rapid succession, came a flurry of skirts, petticoats and pistol shots.

Mr Thomas Fuller fell to the floor and, with one last look at the ceiling, exclaimed...

'I -hate -you....Ca.'

And died.

'Your aim. It was good Miss Westbrooke', said Catherine Barbazon.

'As was yours mademoiselle', commented Lucy Ferrars very dryly. 'Mr Fuller has two shots through him. Was that your cousin whom Miss Westbrooke despatched earlier?'

'It was', said Catherine with a frank look.

'Why', continued Mrs Ferrars, 'you have helped us I cannot well understand. But we must thank you for it.'

'Indeed yes', said Caroline with a surprised expression and cautious half smile, 'I took my own precautions against Mr Fuller. Yet it is quite possible even so that, without your aid, my friend would be dead and myself married to him. Being then amongst the living dead. Was such a boast true? I can scarce believe it.'

Catherine Barbazon looked at her very intently and then fished out two pieces of paper from Thomas Fuller's pockets. Casting a quick eye over both she then passed the first to Lucy.

'Read it to her Mrs Ferrars.'

'I hereby give my full consent', began Lucy, 'to the marriage of my daughter Caroline, who I hereby declare to be the lawful heir to all my wealth and property, to Mr Thomas Fuller and that, upon the said marriage taking place, the Tinterton estates and title shall pass unto the same Mr Thomas Fuller and upon his death to any issue from that union.'

'Is that your father's hand ?', asked Lucy of Caroline.

Miss Westbrooke merely nodded dumbly.

'Well, as Mr Fuller is dead it is now of no consequence as regarding your future. But there are curious things about it. May I be permitted to see the other correspondence Mademoiselle Barbazon?'

Catherine handed it to her. 'You can make sense of that?'

Lucy looked up from the latest coded message. 'With the aid of a pen, paper and five minutes indeed I could. But I rather fancy you can save me the trouble mademoiselle?'

The beautiful young frenchwoman wrote down the translation and passed it across.

meet york black boy. send card. your charlotte.

'I shall leave you now I think' said Catherine Barbazon as Caroline and Lucy exchanged glances, 'for you have much to consider.The landlord here is already aware of what he must do. That the gold I paid him was to keep silent and to remove a body. Now that there are two I suppose he will require a little extra reward.'

'I do have one last question to ask of you mademoiselle', said Lucy.'To satisfy my curiosity.'

'If I can oblige Mrs Ferrars.'

'Was Mr Fuller's pistol, shall we say, 'fit for its purpose?'

Catherine Barbazon laughed as the weapon, aimed at the corpse, sent a third shot into it.

'As you see', she replied and, with a contented smile and two respectful inclinations of her head, promptly then made her way downstairs to pay up.

CHAPTER NINETEEN
'THE BLACK BOY INN'

Three days later Lucy and Caroline were back in rooms at 'The York Tavern'. Since both were in agreement that it was not a time to burden Lord and, particularly, Lady, Lunsford with fresh concerns. For Miss Westbrooke the period had been one not only of distress, but also of evaluation.

'Was it Mr Fuller and Charlotte? Was it he who planned your hanging? If so I am content. But if it was she how can I rest nights while you are yet in peril? Oh when I think',she added, with a very heavy emphasis on that 'think' and laying her head on Lucy's shoulder, 'what might have happened. No sister could be more precious to me. Though as to yourself ' she added, twisting her head about to look up at Mrs Ferrars, 'you have one of those already.'

'Hmm. One minute of your company is of more value to me than a lifetime with her' answered Mrs Lucy Ferrars both honestly and contemptuously .But before Miss Westbrooke had the opportunity to respond to this accolade the two women were interrupted by a knock at the door. The servant had brought the expected message from Catherine Barbazon.That young lady had, a little to Lucy's surprise, accompanied them in the coach to York along with her mother the countess and had promised to arrange a meeting with Charlotte Cantlemere.

When Lucy and Caroline walked into the side room of the 'Black Boy' and found a table in the corner it seemed as if every head in the room and in the passageway beyond it was turned their way.Not even sober clothes would have much lessened Miss Westbrooke's likelihood to attract attention, so that the effect of a striking, very expensive and highly fashionable vivid red and white 'spencer' worn over a white gown and topped off with a stylish matching bonnet can easily be appreciated. Privately Mrs Ferrars, more quietly decked out in various shades of blue and grey, considered such ostentation a little unwise, particularly in the area of the Water Lanes. But even Lucy would never have presumed to say so. Especially since the famous incident at Lady Handforth's. Where of course, in case the reader is not familiar with the affair, the opinion was candidly expressed by the hostess that 'Miss Westbrooke your white gown, bonnet and shawl are most ill suited for my picnic.' Following Caroline's instant and furious exit, Margaret Handforth's social circle was permanently halved and every girl in Bath thereafter who wanted to be thought smart wore nothing but white for picnics the whole summer! Tonight however the all too audible fashion comments from members of her own sex upset Caroline not at all and it took the approach of a serving maid to turn an air of enormous self satisfaction to one of surprise. Soon to be followed by open mouthed astonishment. Nor could Caroline easily be blamed for that. Since Lucy was also little calmer.But there was no mistake in spite of second looks. That servant really was Catherine de Traile!'

'Pray do not stare so hard Miss Westbrooke. Your eyes do not deceive you', whispered Catherine and then she looked at Lucy. 'Mrs Ferrars.'

Lucy now spoke out clearly. 'Two glasses of madeira. And look quick about it girl. My friend and I are in much need of refreshment. Then, perhaps, we shall take some food.'

'Yes ma'am. Very good ma'am' replied Catherine, just managing in her bobbed curtsey to keep a straight face and, as she departed, Caroline motioned ever so slightly with her head to the figure approaching them.

'Why... Caroline...Mrs ..Mrs Ferrars. What do you here?' said an evidently flustered Charlotte Cantlemere, casting as she did so her own eyes over Miss Westbrooke's impressive ensemble.

'We might ask the same of you Miss Cantlemere' replied Lucy. 'You have come here alone?'

'To meet with a gentleman I fancy' added Caroline, now looking Charlotte slowly up and down. That yellow pelisse is very elegant. With a fine bonnet to match I see. Are you going away?'

'I - well yes. I am meeting someone. My mother does not

approve. So we meet here. He is exceedingly handsome.'

'Will you not tell us his name? Come now Charlotte. To have won your affections. Who is this most fortunate young man?'

'Mr Thomas Fuller' replied Miss Cantlemere coldly, annoyed that a social inferior like Lucy Ferrars had the presumption to call her by her christian name.

'Excuse me' said Caroline, yet more frostily. 'I will ask the maid what has happened to our Madeira.'

'You may be seated Mrs Ferrars' said Charlotte in a most superior tone to Lucy, who had also got up.

'Thank you no. I prefer to stand and wait for the return of my friend Miss Westbrooke.'

'I am not unaware' continued Charlotte in a voice of self satisfied sympathy,'of the fact that Mr Fuller has taken certain liberties in criticising Caroline's appearance.'

'Miss Westbrooke's appearance I think you mean.'

'If you insist upon it', Charlotte answered irritably. 'But I have scolded him. Of course her gowns are very fine. Too fine perhaps in some eyes. For certain occasions that is all. Not my own thoughts of course. And, whilst her hair is also not so very fashionable at present, I do understand her reluctance to crop it I suppose.'

'Yes just so. I can understand those things too. Not least because fashions may quick change back again. But you spoke, did you not, of a scolding of Mr Fuller? When was that Miss Cantlemere?

'Why today. This very morning. On Pavement.'

'Indeed? That is most interesting. Mr Fuller must be a remarkable gentleman.'

'Thank you for that Mrs Ferrars' said Charlotte, summoning up a company smile for someone she completely despised. 'I do believe him to be so.'

'Yes indeed. Remarkable. That is the only word for it. For to be seen on Pavement conversing with you this morning Mr Fuller is the first man since the Lord Jesus to have risen up from the dead. Pray explain to me then how myself and Miss Westbrooke can see his body in London three days past and yet you can talk with him today.'

Charlotte Cantlemere's composure, so carefully reconstructed with Lucy's help, now began to retreat into uncertainty and confusion. She had lost and the defeat was turned into a rout with the arrival of Caroline. Who had, perceived by Lucy but not by Charlotte, been carefully listening in the company of Catherine de Traile from behind a side wall. Catherine herself, carrying a bundle, followed on a few moments later.

'I... can explain. Caroline. I.. I ..' faltered Charlotte Cantlemere.

'Miss Westbrooke if you please', replied Caroline haughtily.'Mrs Ferrars, that is 'Lucy', is permitted such an intimacy. You are not. Deny if you dare that it was you, with, I have no doubt, your lover's contrivance, who plotted first my friend's death by hanging from a false accusation of murder and then, when that was foiled, by a pistol shot.'

'Pray do not raise your voice ', snapped Charlotte, aware that Caroline's words were now compelling almost as much attention as her appearance had done before.

'How DARE you presume to tell ME what to do!', shouted Miss Westbrooke. 'Let everyone hear just what you are. Mr Fuller was your lover and he was a traitor. So just what does that make you?'

'If I am a traitor's lover you are a traitor's daughter' replied Charlotte with a sneer.

'No she is not. You are a liar Miss Cantlemere. And, unless we get the truth this night, you shall hang for it.'

Charlotte spun round to gaze into the eyes of Lord Minto, who had been at the card table with his back turned. In an instant, before she could even begin to gather her wits, Minto's two companions got up and took her, struggling, by each arm. It did their prisoner's spirits no good at all now to observe that, under their long cloaks, the men wore the uniform of the king's militia. Desperately she summoned up all on a final throw of the dice and screamed out her demands.

'Let me go this instant. I am Lord Cantlemere's daughter. If you do not I will have you whipped. Whipped do you hear. Let - Me - Go.' With the last of these three short words Charlotte attempted suddenly to break free. But it was in vain and, as the hold upon her became yet tighter she simply had to listen.Lord Minto, watchful for any signs of the sympathetic aid she had been courting, barked out his instructions to the onlookers.

'These men are soldiers in the militia and this woman has consorted with a traitor. So, if any of you wish to be still considered loyal subjects of King George you will leave this room and allow her to be quizzed.' Not surprisingly the room was soon emptied of all save himself, Charlotte Cantlemere and her guards, Lucy, Caroline Westbrooke and Catherine de Traile.

'Now Miss Cantlemere', began Minto. 'What can you tell us?'

'Nothing. I do not believe you anyway. Thomas is alive', said Charlotte with a defiant half laugh.

'Do not add folly to your other faults', replied Lord Minto. 'He is dead.'

'Who killed him then and how? ' Charlotte countered with a provocative sneer. 'Miss Westbrooke? With a hairpin?'

'I did', lied Lucy. 'Shot him. Straight through the heart. And believe me nothing would give me greater pleasure than to do the same to you. However I dare say the noose will content me. If England seems a calm pond there be plenty of well born scum like you Miss Cantlemere that float upon its surface and the worst hovel and the lowest whore about here in The Water Lanes is too good to be infected by your company.I have long known of your opinion of me and that, like Mr Fuller, you consider me no lady. But my origins have some advantages over yours.They allow me a certain freedom in behaviour. To do something now that I have wanted to do for a very long time.'

An enraged Charlotte wiped Lucy's spittle from her cheek. 'I will make you pay for that you low born..'

'Take care what you say' interrupted Mrs Ferrars smoothly, 'for I have a great longing, by way of a change, to spank the other cheek. Your pardon for the interruption my lord.'

'Not at all Mrs Ferrars', said Minto. 'You have a little satisfaction?'

'A little yes. Thank you my lord.'

'Oh you are most welcome to it. Now. We shall proceed to other things. Who was it that you saw on Pavement Miss Cantlemere? Who gave you the message? Which you thought to come from Mr Fuller?'

'Mademoiselle Barbazon's brother', replied Charlotte sullenly.

'Charles Barbazon?' asked Lord Minto.

'Yes. He is not here though if that is what you think.'

'No I know that. He will be somewhat delayed. Being now most safely locked up and awaiting execution. Why were you to meet with him?', concluded Lord Minto and choosing to ignore the expressions of surprise upon the faces of every woman present.

'To go to London and meet with Thomas. It cannot be long now.'

'What cannot?'

'The invasion of course', answered Charlotte scornfully. 'With Lord Nelson dead who can command the fleet. England is lost. And you all with it.'

'Oh Admiral Nelson', said Lord Minto steadily, 'set sail quite safely from Portsmouth. Thanks in no small measure to the quick wits of Mrs Ferrars. Ask Miss Westbrooke if you do not believe me.'

Caroline nodded. 'It is true. I say that for the sake of our past dead friendship if it will convince you.. Mr Fuller too is dead.'

'But - you are - no- you are not going to kill me? My father..'

'Is aware of your treachery my lady', said Minto sternly, finishing off Charlotte's sentence before she could appeal.

'But I can explain' said Miss Charlotte Cantlemere as demurely as she could manage while looking from hard face to hard face. 'Thomas - Mr Fuller that is - promised me marriage you see. If I would help him. I was given to understand that Mrs Ferrars was to be imprisoned and kept from meddling. Mr Ferrars was in full agreement anyway.He had some debts. From keeping his wife in comfort he said. This way he would be free of her. One who tries to poison her husband is good grounds for divorce at the least by Act of Parliament and there were witnesses willing to say as much. But Lord Cottam', continued Charlotte, suddenly dropping the demure for the bitter and angry tone, 'proved to be as false as his supposed wealth and Margaret Bellingham is a two faced snake. There is only one person she would have changed her mind for. I know that now. May you be damned in hell Caroline Westbrooke for what you have done to me. I have been cruelly used.'

'To be cursed by you is high praise indeed', replied Caroline so calmly that every face except Charlotte Cantlemere's shot her a look of admiration.

'And Miss Westbrooke has good cause to curse you also', said Catherine de Traile icily as she went on the attack. 'Your views and those of Mr Fuller upon her are well known. Was not the plan that he should extract a promise from Viscount Westbrooke in return for keeping a secret. A promise to marry his daughter and to take all her inheritance? You have a blabbing mother. And what was next Miss Cantlemere? Was it not then to be that, after Bonaparte's invasion was successful, Miss Westbrooke should accompany her father to the guillotine? So that you might become the next lady of Tinterton Manor?'

'How did you hear of this?', answered a taken aback Charlotte hesitantly.

'From my friend. Miss Rebecca Frobisher. For she was discovered and then bound and gagged by Mr Fuller. But stabbed by you Miss Cantlemere.Your gown was spattered with her blood. But you could not find it afterward could you in your room that evening? So you searched the grounds of Dufton Park.Your maid there took the best of care with it though. I was that maid. Just as 'Belinda'. who was dismissed by Countess Arcachon, was Miss Rebecca. But of course you knew that. You see Mrs Ferrars', continued Catherine turning Lucy's way, 'when you were taken away Rebecca made her own enquiries and they led her and myself to York. We had agreed that I would stay at the 'Black Swan' and find out what I could from there while she sought service at Dufton Park. When I learned from the sister of one of the other maidservants there that 'Belinda Tansey' had been dismissed and when Rebecca did not, as she would have done, come to me at the 'Black Swan' I became suspicious and, with the assistance of my new acquaintance, then offered my own services at Dufton. So what happened Miss Cantlemere?', concluded Catherine to Charlotte. 'Where is my friend Miss Frobisher?'

Before Charlotte Cantlemere could begin her reply Catherine picked up the bundle she had brought with her into the room and, having unwrapped it, handed the bloodstained gown it had contained across to Caroline.' I think you will recognise that Miss Westbrooke?'

Caroline nodded.

'Where you will never find her' came Charlotte's proud answer. 'At the bottom of the River Ouse and weighted down with more stones than Micklegate Bar. Thomas always had his suspicions of her. But my gown proves nothing at all. I am innocent. Innocent. Was I not found bound and gagged that very afternoon? Or have you forgot that?'

'Not at all' replied Catherine in such a tone of voice that Charlotte felt her rising hopes of escape evaporating with each word. 'Bound and gagged by Mr Fuller at three in the afternoon. Yet observed by me four hours before drinking coffee with him and very deep in conversation.'

Caroline looked at the bloodied dress she held and then turned to Lord Minto glancing at his pistol.

'I made a vow sir. Will England give me leave to keep it?'

'She will Miss Westbrooke', he replied softly, handing her the weapon.

After Caroline had stared at Charlotte Cantlemere and thrown the weapon aside with a despairing cry of vexation Minto patted her arm.

'Do not distress yourself. Miss Frobisher would understand. A nature such as yours shrinks from such a task - and she loved you for it. As indeed do others. One more even, I fancy, than you suppose. For I have a letter here.'

'My very dearest daughter', it began.

'I pray that you may forgive me for your anxieties and distress and I seek refuge only in that a marriage which I know was totally repugnant in your eyes could never have taken place. Mr Thomas

Fuller discovered himself to be my natural son and indeed I had an affair of passion with Mrs Fuller which was widely known and talked of while married to my first wife. But his mother was not Mrs Fuller, who, when I first met her, had a baby daughter, but rather that lady of more comfortable means who, two years after the death of Georgiana, the first Lady Westbrooke, succeeded to that title herself. One year later that happiest of events, your own birth, occurred and now I have the deepest affection and pride in such a daughter as any father might dream of. A brother may not marry a sister and Lord Minto, upon the event of my untimely death, had all the necessary proofs to safeguard both your independence and your inheritance. We live in perilous times my darling, but, if the fates are kind, I look forward to the day when your dear self and your true friend Mrs Ferrars, to whom I also extend the sincere hand of friendship, shall safely pay a visit to Tinterton.

I remain, as always, your most devoted father.'

Caroline had little time to dwell upon this happier view of her surviving parent's actions however because, at the very moment of reading the last words, she felt her arm lightly touched by Catherine de Traile.

'They are here Miss Westbrooke' she whispered. 'the final actors in our play.'

CHAPTER TWENTY

'THE ENGLISH INQUISITION'

'If you will step this way ladies. Miss Cantlemere is awaiting you.'

The key turned in the lock as the maid left. There was no requirement for Catherine de Traile to do more.

As Lord Minto calmly lit the other candlebra from the one that he was holding, Mademoiselle Catherine Barbazon did not seem any more perturbed than he was as the light showed up four soldiers of the militia. But the same could not be said of her companion.

'Good evening Countess Arcachon', said Minto. 'We are not to have the pleasure of your husband's company also? What a pity. There are so many things that I should like to ask him. Does he run at your command? Well no doubt we shall discover that. Miss Cantlemere is unable to aid us there.'

'If you have no further need of me my lord', intervened Catherine Barbazon, 'I can return to my lodgings. York is a poor exchange for London. The Comtesse my mother will accompany me back to the capital on tomorrow's coach.'

'Then we shall not detain you', Lord Minto replied, 'and England is most grateful.'

As Mademoiselle Barbazon made for the door Caroline Westbrooke and Lucy Ferrars took hold of one arm each. The former smiled up at her. Leaving the latter to add words to the gesture.

'Our thanks are due also mademoiselle.'

'English women are paying their country's debt Mrs Ferrars. As to yourself and Miss Westbrooke however, gratitude is reward enough.'

When Catherine had left the inquisition began. That certainly was how it appeared to Caroline who, with her interest and knowledge of history, considered it all somewhat ironic. Queen Isabella had been one of the monarchs at the time of the Spanish Inquisition and been blamed, probably unfairly, since the accounts were given by men, for its excesses? Whether guilty of such charges or not this Isabella anyway was now the one to be sentenced. Nor was the chief prosecutor long in setting about it

'Where is your husband Countess?'

'I swear I do not know Lord Minto', replied Isabella Arcachon looking more to Caroline than him. 'He is often on business in London.'

'Oh yes we know that. He was seen at a house on Gracechurch Street. A house of a known radical and revolutionary. What is more your husband is referred to as 'Count Philippe' both in Parisian society and at Bonaparte's army headquarters. But we also have known for some time that it is a woman, not a man, who is the commander of the evil forces that seek to destroy this nation from within. And to destroy those who might defend it. Miss Cantlemere's plotting against Mrs Ferrars. Mr Fuller's against Miss Westbrooke. Plots too though against Lady Hamilton and Lord Nelson.'

'What can I know of this?' answered Isabella more confidently. 'Bring your proof against me my lord. If you can. Or have you not dreamed it up as yet?'

'I have no need of dreams.' responded Minto. 'Let us consider your situation. You are married to a known supporter of the cause of Napoleon Bonaparte. You dismissed your maid, Belinda, in reality, Miss Rebecca Frobisher, from your service and shortly after welcomed into your home Miss Cantlemere. Why did you speak the name of your maid countess? No one could know of her could they, so why was it of significance? Unless of course someone there, through Mr Fuller perhaps, had discovered exactly who she really was. Then Miss Rebecca's hand is discovered and a mysterious letter is found. Who was in the best position to place that letter there? At a time and place where Miss Cantlemere might easily collect it? But that plan went wrong did it not Countess Arcachon? For your gardener saw it before she did and so it was brought back to you. Knowing of the abilities of Mrs Ferrars and Miss Westbrooke you tried to pass it off as nonsense. Then you proceed to lock these ladies in a room after, I have no doubt, making contact with Miss

Cantlemere who was in the grounds.'

'That would be at about eleven my lord. While we were taking breakfast.'

'Thank you Miss Westbrooke', said Minto, acknowledging this additional information with a far more genial look than the one that now replaced it as he spoke again to Isabella Arcachon. 'At the time these good ladies are kept at Dufton, Duke Robert Lavalle,a well known opponent of Bonaparte, is stopped and murdered on his way to York and then, after Miss Belinda Fuller has made a most impassioned speech distancing herself from all actions of her brother she is stabbed to death. We could never catch our spider spinning her webs from the centre. But a dog will pick up a scent at last. Even that of an insect. A countess deserves a grand stage and that you shall have. A trial and then a most public hanging. Dismissals and murders must be whole not half done Countess Arcachon.Take her away!', he added to two of the soldiers present.

'Well that is that ladies' he added as Isabella, without a struggle, was led out to the waiting carriage. 'Now we have our Queen Rat you shall have your reward. Presented by Mr Pitt himself with a signed promise to that effect. Will you take it Mrs Ferrars?'

Lucy read the brief correspondence and handed it on to Caroline.

'You can return to London by the end of the week?'

Mrs Ferrars nodded. 'Indeed my lord. We shall say an earlier than planned farewell to the Lunsfords. Two more days here at most.'

Back at the 'York Tavern' Caroline went quickly to bed. Preferring not to dwell on the thought that Countess Isabella Arcachon, whom they had once helped to her fortune, was the foremost traitor in England. Lucy was more troubled. Everything that Lord Minto had said, every link he had fashioned seemed to be sound and yet there was something wrong. She turned over and over. Physically and mentally. Until a sound from the courtyard outside made her sit bolt upright and then get up, throw on a cloak and rush into Caroline's room. Shaking her frantically by the shoulders.The sound, too, was still there. If anything even louder than before.

The sound of a cat's insistent 'meiow'.

CHAPTER TWENTY ONE

'IN FOR THE KILL'

Having made the necessary enquiries and sent off a brief message,Lucy, who had developed over the years a little sense of the dramatic, made her request to the landlord of the 'York Tavern' early that morning. In thirty years it was the strangest one that he could recall, but there was little problem in carrying it out and in a couple of minutes 'Meg', the ten year old brown tabby cat, was placed in a large wooden box along with some food and water.To be transferred to her small wickerwork basket later. Mrs Ferrars left the other portion of the task in the capable hands of Miss Westbrooke, who assured Lydia, the landlord's six year old daughter, that her pet would be returned safe and sound. As is the way with small children the girl quickly recognised honesty and kindness and decided that this nice lady was her friend. Something which Caroline fostered by firstly asking Lydia about her doll and then telling her a story.

Lucy was left to contemplate what she had got right and wrong. She was certain now who the Queen Rat was. Yet to catch her would require both a little craft and patience. Her conversation with Sir Arthur Wellesley came to mind. Bonaparte could be beaten by stealth rather than bravado? Had not also Lord Minto referred to herself and Caroline as cats? Very soon it would be time then for three cats to move in for the kill.

Sitting in their rooms later that morning to await the departure of the coach for London, Mademoiselle Catherine Barbazon and her mother the Countess were somewhat surprised when visitors were announced and, upon looking out of the window, yet more so to observe Lord James Minto and soldiers standing in the courtyard. No doubt, thought both women, such mysteries would soon be explained by the owners of those boots which could now be heard clip clopping their way up the stairs.

When Lucy Ferrars and Caroline Westbrooke had entered the room and the latter closed the door behind her, Catherine began to speak.

'You are fortunate ladies to pay us a call before our departure for London. Though we are pleased to see you of course.

'I am afraid that you will be departing alone mademoiselle', answered Lucy carefully, 'for the Countess must remain. How fares your husband madame?' she added, turning to Catherine's mother.

Catherine replied before Countess Barbazon could collect her thoughts. 'He is dead Mrs Ferrars. But please allow me to ask any questions to her in french. My mother's english is not good.'

'Oh I dare say it is good enough' replied Lucy sharply. "Cannot escape' were words she spoke to Miss Westbrooke in Bath. A little more than 'a' or 'the'? And I fancy she has better words yet in her head. So let us not play games with my wits.'

'Very well madame. But Count Barbazon was guillotined. That means he is dead. As my daughter told you.'

'My friend asked you not to fool with her wits. She is not so simple as to suppose that a person with their head cut off can still be walking around', interrupted Caroline angrily, shoulder to shoulder again in every sense with Lucy.

'What then is your meaning Mrs Ferrars?' responded Countess Barbazon.

'The Count's lands, his wealth and his title were, upon his death, assumed by another. That man became Count Barbazon by the consent of Bonaparte. Who better to act as his eyes and ears in England than one supposed to be an emigre? An emigre known here not as the new Count Barbazon. But as Count Philippe Arcachon. He is your husband. Also he is, for the present, to use Miss Westbrooke's words, 'walking around.'

Having completed her explanation Lucy knocked upon the window and waved at the men standing in the courtyard to come upstairs. The two frenchwomen made no move and no words were spoken until the Countess Barbazon was pinioned between two soldiers. Only then did her emotions get the better of her.

'Your time will come ladies. Very soon. But Philippe. Je ne comp - that is I do not understand. How did you know? You are a witch Mrs Lucy Ferrars.'

'I fancied you could speak good english' replied Lucy with a slow smile. 'But the honour belongs to another. It is only fitting to introduce you.'

Moving to the door and opening it, Mrs Ferrars muttered a few words and came back inside carrying the wicker basket. It was a bizarre moment and did not become less so when 'Meg', having sniffed the air to her satisfaction, promptly walked across to Caroline and, after rubbing up against that lady's skirts, curled up at her feet. At which point the animal's interest in matters ceased. But not her importance.

'A fine cat is she not Countess?'

'I suppose so' said Marie Barbazon in response to Mrs Ferrars' question.

'You have met her before. For she has a most distinctive cry. And is most beautiful marked I think. Come. Do not be impolite. Greet her as an old acquaintance.'

'I do not talk to animals. Especially cats. Who I consider to be the very worst of creatures.'

Lucy Ferrars laughed. 'Indeed? Then you are, in every way, the opposite of Miss Westbrooke. 'Meg' has chosen her place most sensibly I dare say! But she is that same beast that followed my friend into the Saxby's ballroom that evening. That animal that you, so quick, did sweep away from Count Arcachon. Why I asked myself? When his own wife did not?'

Countess Barbazon, observed especially keenly by her daughter, made no explanation. Which left Lucy loose to supply one.

'Let me tell you then what I believe and if it is near the mark.There was once a young boy. Who was harmed in some

117

way, a dangerous scratch perhaps, by a cat. Because of this he has a fear of all cats thereafter. Or maybe it is a sickness if they touch him? Something of one or of the other, or, perhaps, of both. His wife would know of this. For surely it could not long be concealed even if it were wished to be so? But a new wife maybe is somewhat different. Indeed the Countess Isabella told me that her husband loved all animals. I have no doubt you will deny Count Arcachon has such a fear. But when he is captured it can easy be proved with as many cats as the city of London can provide. I wonder how many might be fitted into one small room with a man locked up? Lord Minto has his instructions from me and your one hope of escaping a noose is to lead us quick to where the Count is hiding. For he is hiding is he not? Tell us Countess. For your own neck.'

'Philippe has a cut. Above the eye. Quite deep.That was a cat. Yes I am his wife. But tell you where he is? Never! He is in waiting. For France. War is coming to England.Your fleet will be defeated.'

'I fancy not',said Lucy, 'but we shall see. As to war though I remember well. For you spoke as much before. War in Bath. A city well inland. You knew, then, of the invasion plans. And believed they would succeed.'

'As they will. Lord Nelson is dead.'

'Not at all Countess', said Miss Westbrooke quietly and firmly. 'He leads our ships. To victory. And with it the end of all your hopes.'

While Caroline was delivering this opinion Lucy opened the door for Countess Barbazon to be led out by the soldiers. After she had left and been bundled into a waiting carriage there was still a half hour remaining before the London coach was due. Some twenty minutes of this time was spent in polite conversation between Lucy, Caroline and Catherine before Mademoiselle Barbazon, standing by the window, turned around with the semblance of a smile. She made her farewells. Walked to the door and opened it. To find her passage barred by one of the two soldiers who had not escorted her mother.like Caroline, Catherine had complete confidence in her powers over the male sex. There were various techniques to suit the occasion though and this one called for the cudgel rather than a knife and fork.

'Move aside', said Mademoiselle Barbazon both loudly and haughtily, and, when they did not, she angrily pushed between them. Only to find herself pushed back inside the room and the door closed behind her. Composing herself and straightening her bonnet Catherine turned to Lucy.

'I do not understand. Why I am so prevented? Pray tell those men I wish to leave for London.'

'You do not understand mademoiselle? I wonder at that. However if you will be seated I can explain it.'

Catherine remained by the door and began to look exasperated. 'The London coach wil soon be departing. We can talk about such matters later.'

Lucy, standing by the window, stared out of it for a few moments and then opened it so that all could clearly hear the clatter of wheels and horses hooves.'You are a little late Mademoiselle Barbazon for that coach now. Will you not be seated?'

'Very well. If I must.' said Catherine a touch contemptuously and shrugging her shoulders.

'Good. Now Miss Westbrooke and myself were set a task. To find a woman who we shall call Queen Rat. It was she who plotted the death of Lord Nelson. And other things. But how was she to be found? Well rats will eat anything. They are even thought to destroy each other by some. That was the key to opening the door. That was your weakness Mademoiselle Barbazon. Queen Rat.'

Catherine laughed and skipped lightly to her feet. 'I had not thought you humorous Mrs Ferrars! Myself? Lord Minto has Countess Arcachon in that part. And what of Miss Cantlemere and my mother? Do you forget them? How many 'queen rats' as you call them, do you require? What is more did I not help to save your life? As for you my dear Miss Westbrooke', she added turning to Caroline, 'you might yet have been married to a man that you detest and still crying over the loss of your beautiful hair. Do I not speak truly?'

Caroline made no response. Leaving that duty to Lucy.

'Oh yes mademoiselle. You helped us that is true and, as we said, we are grateful for it. But why? For friendship? That indeed would mean we owe you much. But no .You helped us to help yourself. Because, by that time, you knew full well that Mr Fuller was a bigger danger to you alive than dead. He talked freely. Boasted. I dare say you had marked his card for death even had he succeeded in his designs at Merton. It was at the Saxby Ball I fancy that his fate was sealed just as surely as that of his poor sister by her honest words.You were that 'Catherine' that was to be warned. Your friends were not so sharp as you however. Not only Mr Fuller, but also his lover Miss Cantlemere. She left a message for Countess Arcachon. Believing, wrongly, that that lady was in your confidence and shall we say 'employ'. But she was not and so we read, after a little teasing out, the message. There is plenty more. But that will be for Miss Westbrooke's ears. I fancy you ordered neither the deaths of Count Lavalle nor Miss Rebecca Frobisher. But neither did you wish to stop them. Mr Fuller's was the hand and his would be the neck. All can be sacrificed at your altar. He, rash and vengeful. Miss Charlotte Cantlemere. Who was so foolish as to be enamoured of a traitor. Even your own mother.You are a true daughter of the revolution. The goddess of Paris. Is that not so?'

Mademoiselle Catherine Barbazon smiled serenely and, for the second time in as many minutes, shrugged her shoulders. 'Of course. I have been called the most beautiful woman in France and I have never met any my equal in wits. Not even you Mrs Lucy Ferrars. It is well known. Napoleon will take a new wife. Who better than I? His eyes desire me more than any other and I work his miracle in England. You will let me leave. Not for that. But because you are english and pay your debts. Is that not so?'

Lucy put out her hands in a gesture of resignation. 'Very well Mademoiselle Barbazon. Miss Westbrooke would not have it otherwise. Though I am somewhat less tidy in such matters, we shall not stop you. You have our word. No soldiers shall detain you. Walk down the stairs and you are a free woman.'

'Thank you Mrs Ferrars', said Catherine adding a little nod of the head and a smug smile in Caroline's direction as she reached the door. Opening it that smile was wiped entirely from her face. Yet again she found herself pushed back inside the room. Not this time by a red coated militiaman. But in the considerably more shapely form of a green gowned Isabella Arcachon. Who carried, in each hand, a fencing sword.

'If you kill me' said Isabella, tossing one of the weapons to Catherine, who caught it neatly by the handle before it hit the ground, 'you may marry your Corsican monster. If not my anger and the ghosts of Miss Fuller, Miss Frobisher and Mademoiselle Lavalle's father will all be satisfied.'

Without any preliminaries Catherine Barbazon suddenly lunged forward, but Countess Arcachon had half expected as much and her neat parry sent the frenchwoman stumbling past her. It was too great a temptation to resist and, en route, the side of Catherine's expensive and highly fashionable light blue dress was neatly sliced open.

'Your petticoats are showing mademoiselle', taunted Isabella, beckoning her forward with her sword. 'Come. Let us see if I can cut up the other side also.'

'That was a - lovely new gown. And -you will pay in - blood for it!' replied Catherine angrily, lunging forward at each pause with a sword thrust. All of which Isabella coolly parried. Before, after another adroit move by Countess Arcachon, Mademoiselle Barbazon lost both her balance and her bonnet.

'You do look most untidy now. What next? How would Bonaparte judge a battle scarred face?'

A furious Catherine got to her feet. But the very thought of losing her precious looks made caution a positive necessity and

121

now it was Isabella that went onto the attack. After two half lunges forward she made another. Faster. Catherine's sword did save all of her facial beauty.

But none of her unprotected stomach.

The darling of Napoleon Bonaparte was dead

Skewered as neatly as meat upon a spit.

CHAPTER TWENTY TWO

'ALL IS LAYERS YOU SEE'

Not at all to Lucy's surprise, Countess Marie Barbazon decided to try to save her neck by delivering up her husband and, when he was captured, the Count did the same by implicating his legal wife. Consequently, with the evidence supplied by each, both were hanged. However we put our cart a little before the horse! Let us return then to the point at which we left Lucy, Caroline and Isabella. All standing around the body of Catherine Barbazon.

After Lucy had called to the soldiers to remove the body Isabella ventured to ask her how she had arrived at the truth. Mrs Ferrars smiled and, when all three ladies were seated, began her explanation.

'I must say that it was most difficult at first. For there were so many actresses, including yourself, who might have played that role. What did soon become clear though was that the Queen Rat would cover her tracks by the actions of others. From the beginning of this affair there were curious happenings which seemed to have no thread between them. My husband disappeared and I was held- on no good ground - until, by my friend here's efforts, I was freed. At the same time Rebecca Frobisher and Catherine de Traile also vanished. I suspected Charlotte Cantlemere from the very beginning of some involvement. She has always disliked me because I am not well born and also, I fancy, because I had displaced her as, shall we say 'Miss Westbrooke's confidante'. I should have given this matter greater weight than I did. For, as we know, it had more to it than injured pride and girlish pique. With myself removed I dare say Charlotte and her lover felt they had the measure of our Miss Westbrooke.'

'I would have wagered they had not' said Isabella, swapping smiles with Caroline and Lucy nodded as she continued.

'So should I. However she had some solid hopes of breaking our friendship. For she believed, no doubt through her mother, that

Viscount Westbrooke wished also to set his daughter free from me. Was she though 'Queen Rat?' I was not inclined to believe it. Even so she was surely more than a small rat and that was made clear when her mother remarked quite forcefully at the Assembly Rooms in Bath that Miss Westbrooke would have to marry. She would have no choice. Viscount Westbrooke's obviously now quite genuine assurances to his beloved daughter that her wishes would always be respected were probably dismissed at the time as social pleasantries and, when Mr Thomas Fuller openly stated here in York that he would be prepared to make her his wife after previous insulting her, another rat was added. I had thought Miss Belinda Fuller a possible Queen Rat, but of course, she most bravely set that notion aside at the Saxby's Ball. Though Miss Belinda's words also sent me a little astray. The 'she' to whom reference was made was present that night to hear it. Charlotte Cantlemere listened and did not talk that evening. You remember Caroline?'

Miss Westbrooke nodded.

'So', continued Lucy, 'I dare say that it was she who told Mr Fuller of the true feelings of his sister. Surely Catherine Barbazon would not involve herself in such small matters? What if Thomas was caught? No, that, I am certain, was Charlotte's doing. All is layers you see.'

'Layers?' questioned Caroline and Isabella also looked a little fogged.

'Yes. One murder, one plot, is the best way to hide another. Rats scurry in all directions. One layer is the common soldier of a plan. Such as Sally Duncan. Paid for her work, as she thought, in money alone. The next is Thomas Fuller. Each 'layer' best protects itself by removing the one beneath when danger threatens. Firstly Thomas should have killed Sally Duncan. When she had delivered the poison, and before it had taken its effect, Sally would walk out of the house to receive her payment. He would arrange her death, hiding the body no doubt, and leave by the same manner he had come. With Lord Nelson dead who would look for a missing maidservant anyway?Unless it be to suspect her of the deed? But as we know it did not succeed. Sally Duncan confessed. What now can Thomas Fuller do?'

'He could have gone to Portsmouth', suggested Isabella 'to carry out the Queen Rat's wishes'.

'Or he could have gone to Lord Minto with what he knew.' posed Miss Westbrooke.

Lucy gave two respectful glances. One in each direction.

'Both are firm ground in places even if, to my mind, the one requires more courage and the other more cunning than he possessed. Certainly either presented more hope than the course of action he chose. Which was to confess all to Catherine Barbazon. Consider now her situation if you would. Sally Duncan has almost certainly talked. Of Mr Fuller. Who has now come to her. His lover and confidante is also Charlotte Cantlemere, who Mademoiselle Barbazon knew was closely acquainted with Miss Westbrooke. The web she has used to protect herself is in danger of falling so threadbare that its only use will be to trap the spider's legs in flight. So she thinks. Coldly. So coldly I can almost admire it in her I do confess. What happens next I dare say is this. She goes first to Christophe, her cousin, who is of course, like her, a firm Bonapartist. Tells him of the threat that is now not only ourselves but also Mr Thomas Fuller. The pistols are prepared. Together they then meet with Mr Fuller. To set the trap. It is amusing that he said to me while pointing a gun at my head, 'we shall see this little play last until the end.' Now I doubt not, that, had you not prevented it', continued Mrs Ferrars with an intent look at Miss Caroline Westbrooke, 'Monsieur Christophe Barbazon would have played out his part to the last and presented you before us crop haired and in your shift. Nor do I much doubt that his sister would have found some satisfaction in it either for all her 'flowered' compliments at the Saxby's' reception.So we have the shooting. It was safe for Mademoiselle Barbazon to glance away That let matters take their course you see. Either, she imagined, Mr Fuller would kill Miss Westbrooke and I, also, would be killed, or Mr Fuller would die and, as she saw him fall, she supplied the second shot to establish her innocence. Mr Fuller was always to be shot anyway though by her I fancy. He had become too dangerous for his own good. Of course we saved her the trouble.'

'Was it she also that promised me in marriage to that detestable creature?' asked Caroline.

Mrs Ferrars shook her head. 'Oh Mademoiselle Barbazon read your father's letter. But I am bound to say there, somewhat in her defence, that it did not interest her at all. 'Promised by C'. How misled I was there. For the word itself should have held my thoughts. Mr Fuller had made his 'promise' of marriage to another. Who better to make a promise than one who most sure believed that it would not be of lasting consequence? It was Charlotte Cantlemere who had made the promise. Agreeing that Thomas Fuller could marry you. Only for you, as Miss de Traile told us before, to die later. But Charlotte's fate too became sealed with her own letter to Thomas Fuller. Catherine Barbazon read that also and so decided to accompany us, her 'new friends' that she had helped to save, to York. To make sure that her own innocence was given still greater weight.'

Miss Caroline Westbrooke, while admiring of her friend's deductions, wriggled, just a touch impatiently, in her seat.

'Yes I see your reasoning Lucy. But how did you know it was Mademoiselle Barbazon that was Queen Rat and not the countess - Isabella - here?'

Lucy put out her hands.

'The message?. That which you, countess, handed over to us? 'Catherine must be warned.' I fancied that someone, most likely Charlotte Cantlemere, had mistakenly thought you part of the conspiracy. As we know she had changed her mind before about you. Deciding to stay at Dufton Park as your guest. Now she could only fancy your involvement if someone close to you was known to be working for Bonaparte. Who better then than Count Arcachon? Mademoiselle Barbazon first came a little under my suspicion when I remembered his attentions to her at the ball. When my mind turned also as to how a Queen Rat might best protect herself I recalled a number of other things about her too. Of how she quick changed the conversation from the war that evening in Bath. Of how she alone

126

was not known by the Lavalles. The most likely reason for that was an absence from society. Strange indeed, especially for one so beautiful. Yet not so strange if other matters prevented it. Also Catherine Barbazon had, had she not Caroline, a great air of command that day when she so easy arranged the murder of Thomas Fuller?.'

'Indeed yes' replied Miss Westbrooke. 'Almost as if she enjoyed the task.'

'Exactly' said Lucy, 'and when she could so cold hearted not shed a tear for her own cousin and spoke not a word either to save her mother I was certain she deserved the title of Queen Rat. Indeed Mademoiselle Cathcrine Barbazon', concluded Mrs Ferrars drily 'for all her great beauty and fine airs is not someone I shall grieve over.'

'And as to myself?' said Isabella. 'was I in danger?'

'I fancy not' said Lucy. 'For when the truth was known to all where your loyalties lay it was too late. You had dismissed 'Belinda', Miss Rebecca, for her insolent remarks. Pray do not blame yourself for her death, for Rebecca had.made quite sure that you would do so. She needed to do her own work. Work which caused her murder. Charlotte Cantlemere had carefully left the secret message under the stone for you to find and spoke with Mr Fuller on the subject. Only, too late, for her,to realise that your words about giving 'Belinda' notice had no hidden meaning in them. I had noted by the way upon that little matter that the paper,although both neat written and folded, was also torn. This had not happened I fancied in the act of putting it under the stone.That word 'placed' I remarked upon. It was quite deliberate and the tear was on an inside fold. So how might it most likely have been done? Surely by the writer being surprised in some way? This would hardly matter outside of Dufton Park, but within its confines? That would lead suspicion onto someone already within the house. Suspicion that would deepen should they disappear. As to yourself I was inclined to be convinced of your innocence in any plots by the newspaper. For surely, if you was concerning yourself for ill in my affairs, you would not be so open in expressing it? I therefore presumed it was meant for me to find as pledge of friendship. The only matter I have not been able to tie up neat is why you locked the two of us up so long. I can only suppose it to be for our protection.'

Isabella nodded. 'I saw a movement in the bushes. Before you came down to breakfast. The grounds are extensive and I did not wish harm to come to either of you until they had been fully searched. I guessed that you would be suspicious and could only hope that the newspaper I had placed in your room would -if I might say it - be read correctly. When I went to the window again at breakfast, I saw the ghost again in the gardens and could not be satisfied of your safety.'

Lucy stared at her. So surprised was Mrs Ferrars that she required three quite separate confirmations. 'You say you saw the ghost again? In the garden? While Caroline and I were taking our breakfast?'

'Yes. Of course it was Miss Cantlemere. Why she chose to..'

Isabella stopped mid sentence as Lucy put up a hand.

'It was not Charlotte Cantlemere. For we know from Miss de Traile that, at that time, she was in York.'

'Why yes that is so' said Caroline. 'But it cannot have been Catherine Barbazon either I think? Mademoiselle Lucie Lavalle said the whole family were snakes. But would she chance being caught and anyway how would she arrange it all? Moreover why? She had nothing to gain as I see it from frightening either Isabella or myself. To be a ghost is hardly hiding in the shadows is it? Especially in a dazzling gown.'

Mrs Ferrars smiled. 'No indeed. I agree with you. It was not Catherine Barbazon. But that conversation. Snakes. Watching and waiting. Striking in any direction. Well well. We must have words with Lord Minto. Before this evening is upon us.'

CHAPTER TWENTY THREE

'QUITE A COLLECTION'

That night at the Theatre Royal in York was to prove a memorable one for everyone. The play had been splendidly acted. William Shakespeare was as popular in 1805 as he had been in his lifetime, even if, from time to time, Georgian producers felt the need to alter endings. Not that there was any need to do so in this instance. For what more appropriate play than 'Henry the Fifth' given England's peril from across the Channel? The Battle of Agincourt was, accordingly, greeted with cheers and the actor playing Henry duly milked the applause. Even so it was clear to anyone with knowledge of acting talent that the star in this production was not England's famous warrior king but rather the sweet tempered Princess Katherine. She of the fluent french and delightfully halting english. Supreme in this performance, she fully deserved her accolades and, having enjoyed them, retired to her room backstage which she alone occupied. Or so she believed. Until, sitting down, she heard the key turn in the lock. It was Lucy Ferrars, of the three visitors, who spoke first.

'Good evening Miss Blandford. A fine performance.'

'Thank you Mrs Ferrars', said Louisa calmly. 'I am pleased you found it so for the role is not an easy one for me.'

'I can understand that difficulty', Lucy responded, 'for Princess Katherine is what she appears to be.'

'I do not think I fully comprehend your meaning.'

'You understand it very well Miss Blandford. You are a deceiver without equal. A deceiver moreover who works for Bonaparte. If you know aught of my reputation you must allow that I am not likely to be very easy duped.'

Louisa Blandford laughed scornfully as she took off her headdress and, pushed back her black curls. 'If that were so why, pray, has it taken you so long to trap me? Your wits have become dulled madam. I work for Britain. Ask Lord Minto.'

'Have I said that you do not?', countered Lucy and Louisa's eyes narrowed. 'Do not spout of loyalties. Save your breath. The portrait of Princess Katherine has been pretty well drew by you tonight and I would not wish it spoiled by smudges and splashes. I can see it now clear enough. Lord Minto needed an actress to learn a part for a new play he had written with Lord Brocklehurst. Let us call it 'Deliver up the Bonapartists'. A clumsy title and I am sure Miss Westbrooke or yourself could think up a better. For scholarship was never my strongest card. Anyway what happens I fancy is this. You leave the theatre company you are with and enter Bath and London society. To learn all that is possible about french families. Making the most useful acquaintance of Mademoiselle Lucie Lavalle you gain that most honest and estimable young lady's trust and, from her, learn of the hostility of the Lavalles to the Barbazons. One of these families then is firm for Bonaparte. To determine which you write two messages. Both are the same and both are delivered upon that evening reception in Bath attended by many including Lord Minto, Miss Westbrooke and myself. Mademoiselle Barbazon receives one, Mademoiselle Lavalle the other. All must then go to York. All are hounds and hares.'

'This is nonsense. I will hear no more of it', Louisa Blandford replied angrily and made to get up to leave the room. Lucy wasted no time on niceties and, catching hold of a good handful of Miss Blandford's hair, pulled her down again so hard that it made the young woman cry out in pain.

'You must listen to Mrs Ferrars', said Lord Minto, taking a pistol from the pocket of his long coat, 'or I will shoot you where you sit.'

'Thank you my lord' said Lucy, now releasing her hold upon Louisa. 'Now Miss Blandford. How may you lose? Lord Minto is paying you to aid Britain and the Countess Barbazon and her daughter likewise to aid Bonaparte. All the golden eggs are in your basket and travelling up to York. The message is clever. Written in such a manner as to appear hidden and therefore trustworthy, yet easy enough to be understood by anyone with competent wits. You could, no doubt, have supplied a wordy prod or two, but I dare say Mademoiselle Barbazon and her mother needed that no more than Lord Minto did. So what occurs next? I shall sketch my view of it and you may tell me later if there is much in the way of error. '

Louisa Blandford stared straight ahead with what was, Lucy keenly noted, still a remarkably composed expression.

'So', continued Mrs Ferrars, 'using your talents you travel in Lord Minto's carriage disguised as a militia soldier. A soldier who, in spite of the warm weather and, shall we say, the relaxed nature of duties of which other men took full advantage, never removed his shako? For, regarding you now, we may see indeed the great importance of that headpiece. Given the task once in York of watching over myself and Miss Westbrooke you then, with his lordship's assistance I fancy, gained entry to Countess Arcachon's home at Dufton Park. Is that not so my lord?' .

Minto nodded and gave a guarded smile. 'She came to me saying that she knew Charlotte Cantlemere was false and believed Countess Arcachon to be also .When Miss Cantlemere arrived at Dufton Miss Blandford was in attendance as one of the maids.'

'Next Miss Blandford', said Lucy, 'having entered Dufton you spent considerable time when not at your duties finding your way about. Then you placed a skull, part of your theatrical baggage no doubt, for Countess Arcachon or her servants to find. Hoping that it might lead, as indeed it did, to that lady requesting the company of Miss Westbrooke and myself and so leading us away from York. That was very important was it not?'

'I have no idea as to your meaning.'

'Very well. I shall explain it. Not to you, who coolly lie and need no answer, but to my friend and to Lord Minto.They shall be your judges.'

Louisa Blandford started and looked at the speaker. Before, yet again, that composed expression settled itself down on her face.

'You speak as if I had committed a crime of some sort. I invite you to prove it. Come. What little wisdoms have you now? What malice? Let us hear it all', concluded Louisa mockingly and cocking her head to one side.

'I am glad to observe' responded Lucy to this behaviour, 'that your neck is getting practice for being broke. There is one person you feared. One person that had guessed your loyalties. Loyalties to money only and not country or cause. That man was Duke Robert Lavalle. In Bath he had warned Miss Westbrooke, for whom he had much regard, against travelling to York. So you took Charlotte Cantlemere into your confidence and told her that, were the duke to be allowed to talk, his words would send her, her lover Mr Thomas Fuller and also Countess Barbazon and her daughter all to the gallows. Now Mr Fuller I am certain, was the man that shot the duke. But it takes two to hold up a carriage and Mademoiselle Lucie said as much later when we questioned her. Miss Cantlemere could not have accomplished all that was required in the time. But a good actress, especially one so good as to become a soldier, could have done. An actress needs costumes of course. Which she must keep in a separate trunk for her own plays. We had a good search of your rooms at 'The Black Swan' Miss Blandford. But how stupid a notion that was. For a careless or inquisitive maid might get the idea to open it. Where safer then than a theatre? Where dangerous costumes might mix in with all the others.'

Louisa now sat very still as Lucy walked across to the box at the side and lifted out clothes item by item.

'Quite a collection', began Mrs Ferrars. 'Here, for example, is a dark coat answering the very same description given by Mademoiselle Lucie of that worn by one of the highwayman. The one that held a pistol to her head while her father was being shot. What a cold hand that was - and what a good disguise too to one who had been your friend? And here no doubt is a maid's garb for Dufton Park. And is not this Miss Westbrooke', added Lucy as she held up for Caroline's inspection a tattered gown, 'that worn by the beggarwoman at Castlegate Postern? The beggarwoman who, in effect, set us on our path to London?'

'It is indeed', said Caroline giving Louisa Blandford a bitter look that seemed to have no effect at all. 'But why should she give us that message? Why not just destroy it? I do not understand.'

'Huh! That does not surprise me in the slightest' said Louisa with a contemptuous little laugh 'and I have no intention of lighting up your dimness.'

'Well' continued Lucy, fishing out another garment from the box, 'this may give some light for Miss Westbrooke. Is it not the same which was worn by a certain ghost? And is not this', she added, holding up a very lifelike white mask with vivid green eyes, 'the face of terror which you saw?'

Caroline nodded.

'Just as I supposed. A ghost who knew the house and who had a stong sense of the dramatic. Deny Miss Blandford all the fine accomplishments of character we will but never craft and guile. After Miss Cantlemere's departure and with, no question ,her full assent, Miss Louisa Blandford hides herself away. That ghost never walked down no stairs. Nor up them did it Miss Blandford? Our friend here', continued Lucy staring hard at Louisa's impassively stony face, 'had hidden herself away in Miss Westbrooke's room and, when she, understandably frightened, then rushed into my own, the 'ghost' was delivering a similar scare to Countess Isabella Arcachon. Then departing to walk into one of the rooms beyond. For which, no doubt, she had also succeeded in obtaining a key. When the countess then, again as might have been presumed, made her exit to warn ourselves of the spectre it became no more. Changed into a serving maid. Who probably remained in the room opposite until the next morning. How was all this done? Well, as so often, it was you Miss Westbrooke who showed that to me.'

'I did nothing.'

'Oh indeed you did. You remarked later, most decidedly, upon how narrow was the passageway. As you said it was quite impossible for any lady in a wide gown to make her way down it without considerable inconvenience and, when I further quizzed you as to the likely date of its construction you ventured it to be probably of the time of Queen Elizabeth. My knowledge of history is far inferior to your own, but even I recall sufficiently from my uncle Mr Pratt that it was a period of religious persecution and that the north of England had many catholics who must be hidden away. In a priests hole. Which, I venture, lies behind the fireplace in Miss Westbrooke's room? Or can be accessed from the same.'

'I congratulate you Mrs Ferrars' said Louisa Blandford 'and it would appear that you have at least some right to your reputation. Though there are some small matters in which you are in error.'

'Indeed?'

'Yes. Yet they may prove somewhat of an irritant to your pride. I came not from behind the fireplace in Miss Westbrooke's room but rather the tallboy. I am surprised that she did not take note that it was pulled out a little way from the wall. Though as her bed was upon the other side maybe I am a little harsh in judgement there. I had Miss Cantlemere to help me move it of course before her own mysterious disappearance. Also, while I did change into a serving maid's attire, when the Countess had entered your room I simply walked back into hers. No one had, as yet, come upon the scene and I had time to hide myself away once more in the secret passage for the night. I knew that the countess always left the door to her room unlocked when she went downstairs for breakfast. Anyway that is all of no matter. There is a secret passage linking all and leading, as you suggest,right the way down the passage and into Countess Arcachon's room. Where the fireplace is, indeed, the entrance. When I discovered all that the desire to make two nightly visitations and not one was too pressing to resist. It was rashness I later regretted. Not for the danger of discovery so much, for my plans were well laid, even so far if necessary as to the picking of locks. But a ghost is not often seen by more than one victim of an evening and, too late, I considered that you Mrs Ferrars might have the wit to see that. Miss Westbrooke, all shrieks shivers and trembles, should really have been quite sufficient in satisfaction', concluded.Louisa with a superior grin at a blushing and nettled Caroline.

Lucy nodded without enthusiasm and held up two clasps which she had been busy unfastening from, as it were, the ghost's gown.

'These clasps are yours?'

'Of course they are' said Louisa Blandford, now showing, for the first time, considerable emotion. 'And do not, pray, damage or steal them. They are pure gold and of a most unusual design. But please I implore you. Give them back to me. They are mine. Bequeathed to me by my mother. I meant no lasting harm to Miss Westbrooke. But to disturb that self satisfaction, however justified...?'

Lucy looked from her to Caroline and back again. Preferring not to analyse too much the mix of sympathies and criticisms.

'I shall honour that request Miss Blandford. If an apology to Miss Westbrooke is paid in return.'

'Thank you Mrs Ferrars. I meet that price', replied Louisa, putting her hands out palms up.

'As you say', interrupted Lucy, giving the clasps a final glance before handing them across to their owner and bypassing Caroline Westbrooke's exasperated look, 'the design and workmanship is truly remarkable. Figures of birds I think?'

Louisa shook her head. 'Not quite. One is yes. A hawk. With a mouse in its talons. But the other is a bat.'

Lucy Ferrars turned her head slowly now to speak to Caroline.

'Do you not recall what Lord Minto told us when we first began this investigation my dear? That someone had been questioned concerning the identity of the Queen Rat and that they had said but one strange word?'

'Yes. Batork. But it makes no sense. Oh I see it now. Not Batork. But bat and hawk. I knew I had seen those clasps before and now I remember. It was upon the miniature of Mademoiselle Suzanne de Poitiers. Small. Very small. But I have an eye for details. Indeed', concluded Miss Caroline Westbrooke proudly, 'I do not always see so dimly as some ignorant people may suppose.'

'That is certain', said Lucy. 'However we can make sure that the miniature is the only record of such a match. For this gown' she added, lifting out the red and gold one we mentioned earlier, 'I shall now take. It belonged to Mademoiselle Suzanne de Poitiers and we can send it later, in ashes, to the memory of its mistress.'

'No. That I will not allow. Tell her to stop Lord Minto.'

Lord James Minto answered Louisa Blandford's words by turning his pistol from her to Lucy.

'Hand the gown to Miss Blandford madam. Or not one penny of the reward will be yours.'

Lucy did as she was told and then turned to question Louisa.

'Why is that gown of such importance Miss Blandford? And how came you by it?'

'Because it was my sister's. Lord Minto knows the truth of it. I', concluded Louisa very proudly ,'am Mademoiselle Catherine de Poitiers.'

CHAPTER TWENTY FOUR

'BITES BETTER FOR THE TEETH'

Lucy turned now to Lord James Minto.

'It is for you to speak my lord. I fancy Miss Blandford, as we knew her, is deceiving us no longer. But can the same be said of you?'

Minto looked as forbidding as he could. A gesture completely wasted upon Lucy Ferrars.

'Remember that you have not yet been paid and are swimming in murky swirling waters. More money than you dreamed of in Devon will be yours if you keep silent on these matters as well as other rewards. I had hoped that you would be content with a fruitless search of Mademoiselle de Poitiers' room at the 'Black Swan'. But indeed you have lived up to your reputation for being both crafty and persistent. So I see that more bunches of sweet grapes must be dangled. Your husband has, for his own safety, been persuaded to petition for a divorce. Needing an Act of Parliament. Which I have a strange feeling will certainly be quickly passed. That is if his wife says nothing of Mademoiselle Catherine de Poitiers. I said to you once before it was hard to be sure of your existence. I advise the same line of thought to yourself and Miss Westbrooke concerning this lady here. If not who knows what might follow? Suddenly all those accusations of murdering a husband might just reappear. Given greater weight with the discovery of his dead body. As for Miss Westbrooke? Well a marriage to someone much older, not at all handsome and with a certain reputation for roughness with women would seem to draw rather closer.'

'Do not threaten me my lord. My father would never agree to that.'

'Dead men have a fine way of keeping silent my dear Miss Westbrooke', said Minto, 'and aunts likewise if needs be. You will marry. Or not. Your choice.'

'I have no choice', replied Caroline 'and, now that I know a little of

Miss Blandford's - of Mademoiselle de Poitiers' - past, it is not quite so unpleasant an oath to keep. But why did you not trust us?'

'Oh I trusted you. And believe me, had you not accepted my terms, I should have trod so slowly and softly as to give you every chance to reconsider. But I had no such faith or sensibilities concerning Mrs Ferrars. Without your efforts she would be in prison still. Was she loyal? We could not be sure and Miss Margaret Bellingham, who you, I am certain, encouraged to give false evidence in order to free your friend, could not be persuaded to admit it.'

Caroline looked as angry as Lucy had ever seen her. 'What have you done to poor Margaret?'

Minto gave a wintry and not unsympathetic smile. "No more than we had to. No lasting damage and nothing to lessen her undoubtedly very giddy attractions for certain gentlemen. But she will be a week or two from dancing yet. Pain though is only of use when the price matches up to a hidden secret. It would seem that we much undervalued her fondness and loyalty toward yourself. So be it. But to return to Mrs Ferrars. If she proved to be either weak or false Miss Louisa here would tell us. Like you she works for money. You would make a fine pair understanding each other so well. Shall I tell them all Miss Louisa?'.

'Pray do so Lord Minto.'

'Very well. This young lady is a traitor to her country. A country that has sent thousands to the guillotine including her own father and sister. Thanks to our own countrymen she escaped to England and has more cause than any here to wish death to all Bonapartists. Two years ago she became an actress and, I think we may all agree, a most accomplished one. She became known to the government and kept her eyes and ears open for us. For gold naturally. Then she went to Catherine Barbazon. To Lucie Lavalle. Even to Philippe Arcachon. Whom she knew had sent her family to the guillotine. A brave act this, for you may well suppose that she could have been recognised. Except that an actress- well I may leave the rest to your imagination. We soon found more work for her too, not just looking over Mrs Ferrars but also because we had knowledge of Mr Thomas Fuller. A boaster and braggart, free with his opinions, especially in his cups. When Miss Cantlemere became his lover roads did begin to converge. Miss Louisa had now left the theatre and stayed, for appearance sake, with our good servant Mrs Hunter who acted as her companion.Then Mrs Ferrars', Minto added to Lucy 'your version of events is of such accuracy that I need not repeat it except so far as to some small explanations and additions.The death of Miss Belinda Fuller she sadly brought upon herself. Louisa observed her leaving her house clutching a note in her right hand. She was followed by her brother, a sly dog indeed, but not so clever as the beggarwoman who, moments before Belinda Fuller was confronted by her brother, pushed her to the ground and seized that paper from her. Whether the approaching Thomas Fuller, who in his rage then stabbed his prostrate sister, had any intent upon following the beggarwoman or not we shall never know because, of course, a crowd was gathering and he needed to make good his escape. As was intended you received the message, though not by the original bearer of it. The rest I fancy is as you supposed. Or have you aught to add 'Miss Louisa Blandford'? Before I thank you for your services to England and Mrs Ferrars, Miss Westbrooke and myself leave you to change out of your dress.'

'One matter only. One regret.'

'What is that pray?' said Lucy as the three visitors made their way to the door.

'Your friend Miss Frobisher .I wish I might have saved her. Miss Fuller also perhaps. But there is a time to strike and a time to wait. They did not know which was which as I did. I have taken french gold as well as english and it bites better to the teeth. For that is Bonaparte's stolen plunder. Stolen from families like mine. I have earned that twice over. I distrust all and hate all displays of affection and display. Even upon occasion' added Louisa with the slightest of smiles to Caroline, 'being a little savage upon the point sometimes.Yet I would not desire us to part as enemies Mrs Ferrars. You are worthy, as I said before, of your reputation.'

'Thank you Miss Blandford' replied Lucy carefully, ' that is an opinion to be valued.'

Louisa turned now to Caroline. 'And as to you Miss Westbrooke?'

'I bear you no lasting ill will and thank you for your regrets as to Miss Frobisher and Miss Fuller. But Duke Lavalle is dead. Nor shall I forget the ghost. I do not care much for teasing at my expense and certainly not from strangers.You will never frighten me in mortal form. 'Miss Blandford'.'

Louisa Blandford, alter ego Catherine de Poitiers, to Caroline's surprise, did not seem at all offended. Indeed, by her smile, very much the opposite.

'I dare say I shall not hazard such a risky stake again Miss Westbrooke. There is more than one type of disguise and I congratulate you upon yours. Frivolity and ferocity. Sensibility and sense. How splendid! You would have been wasted upon either Mr Thomas Fuller or Mr John Saxby I think.'

'Mr Saxby?' replied Caroline puzzled, 'what has he to do with this?'

Louisa Blandford laughed. 'Nothing at all. He is what he appears to be. Unlike any here. Without even a scrap of artifice. The perfect gentleman. Who thinks you so far above him as to turn dreamlike imaginings into absolute truths. Confess it now. Would not marriage to such a doting fawn be almost as repugnant as one to the foxy Mr Fuller?'

'No it would not Miss Blandford. I shall not marry Mr Saxby because I do not love him. But I do respect him. And his feelings for me. Which you do not understand it seems. There is one important difference in our disguises.'

'What is that?' said Louisa with a shrug of the shoulders.

'Why that mine has a heart within it. You have turned yours to hardened gold. There is only one man now that you could happily marry, whether as Miss Louisa Blandford or as Mademoiselle Catherine de Poitiers. And I pity you for it.'

'Indeed? And who might that be?'

'King Midas' answered Miss Caroline Westbrooke, promptly closing the door behind her.

CHAPTER TWENTY FIVE

'BURN BRIGHT ON TOP OF YOUR HILL'

'Lucy.'

'Yes.'

'There are still some things about this affair that I do not quite grasp and, if you would care to look at this list I have made..?'

Mrs Ferrars smiled pleasantly at her friend Miss Caroline Westbrooke seated beside her again on the sofa.They were back in their rooms at Queen Square Bath and she could afford to relax happily now. Not only were herself and Caroline both two thousand pounds each the richer and had received a royal audience, but of far more significance was the news that the Act of Parliament granting her a divorce from Robert had been enacted with such remarkable speed that the ink had hardly had time to dry upon it from composition to resolution! She was a free woman and not one either in need of a man unless it be for love or recreation.That marriage would be as if it had never been and sound business sense would supply what might offend any delicate vestiges of sensibility. What was more her impecunious husband's obligations to her had been taken over by Lord Cantlemere. In return for the life of his daughter. Charlotte had used every trick in the book from tears to tantrums and strutting to simpering to plead her case. However, since her reward was to become the wife of a man twice her age and of considerably lower social status out in the West Indies, Mrs Ferrars considered further punishments had yet to come.

'Indeed?', replied Lucy adding extras for Caroline to the smile such reflections had brought. 'What, pray, are they? I am surprised that you also have not tied up all. Your writing I am certain will be most neat as always, but I should prefer those thoughts read out.'

'Well in part the questions relate to myself. Though there are other matters also.'

'Let us first consider then those of which you are the centre.'

'I have two. No, three perhaps in a way', said Caroline Westbrooke studying her writing carefully, 'and they are simply put. Why was Mr Fuller so very insistent that I alter my gowns and, yet more so, to cut off my hair and why also did Mr Saxby, before so shy, become particularly pressing in his desire to marry me?'

'I shall answer the last first for it is easiest done' replied Lucy. 'Miss Louisa Blandford as we must regard her, considered him a gentleman entirely without deep designs and I agree. As I said to you before he is, or fancies himself, in love with you. Certainly you informed him that you could not return such a sentiment. Perhaps propriety should have stopped him. That it did not, and that he was prepared to declare his devotion so honestly and openly, thus risking your permanent displeasure, should not be counted against him. Though that must be your decision.'

'I was a little vexed. Since I had... But that is no matter. If he had no other purposes I am pleased. Mr Saxby has many good qualities and I wish him well. Even if that is not enough to lose my independence for.'

'Quite so', said Lucy nodding. 'I also consider Mr Saxby to be, in the main, a most estimable gentleman. Not a description I would give to Mr Fuller. However to begin on I did imagine that his insults toward you were exactly that and with no more malicious purpose. Such a view was merely supported by his comments upon your gown. For Miss Stott, if you recall, had told us of his opinion of hers on the same subject. Yours were too ornate and hers too simple. When one also adds Anne Lunsford's memories of snails on white muslin no more might be supposed than an especially strong teasing of ladies. Your hair though proved a different matter entirely and I should have put a far greater weight upon that issue. Upon the occasion of the quarrel at Grant House he would not, even at the last, depart without telling you once again to cut it. Miss Eleanor Stott led me a little astray at Fawkes House there. For, if you recall, he had also made criticism of her long hair. Probably merely to cause annoyance or embarrassment. However with yourself the matter was

142

of more malice. Your head was to be shaved not cropped. Not a change of appearance then for fashion, personal whim or even a teasing satisfaction, but rather one of humiliation. He was to perform the task himself and evidently relished the prospect. Short of branding upon the face it is hard to imagine an alteration in appearance to cause you greater distress. I, too late, then realised his deep dislike of you and, from what we have learned since from Viscount Westbrooke, there was reason for it.'

'Oh Lucy. All my lovely hair', replied Caroline, fingering the same several times, before, with an embarrassed blush, she continued. 'I feel so ashamed to think of such things though when remembering Duke Lavalle and our dear Rebecca. What is a shaven head compared to them?'

'Why?' said the matter of fact Lucy somewhat to Miss Westbrooke's surprise. 'Your hair, as anyone could easy guess at, is very precious to you. Would sacrificing it have saved anyone's life? No. Mr Fuller had his own plans which were of little interest to Mademoiselle Barbazon and none at all to Louisa Blandford. Who, as you stated yourself, admired your tresses. An honest enough remark I dare say and another little difference I rather forgot.'

'But Charlotte Cantlemere, that she wolf', said Caroline with real venom as she remembered the phrase from Shakespeare, 'knew of his designs. And at least helped Mr Fuller to murder Rebecca and bury her body without either sympathy or ceremony. I hope that planter husband of hers makes her work hard in the fields and she suffers agonies for it.'

'I fully share that desire. Yet I do not fancy that Miss Cantlemere, however great her other sins, had any wish to shave your head. That was entirely Mr Fuller's notion. What, pray, are your other questions?'

'Oh they are here somewhere. Ah yes', added Miss Westbrooke shuffling her papers. 'On this page. Why did Mr Fuller consider Isabella- Countess Arcachon - to be the finest of her sex and what made you suspect Count Arcachon of any involvement? Oh yes and there is this. Why should Catherine Barbazon accuse Mademoiselle

Lucie Lavalle and her family of taking Bonaparte's gold?'

'Three good questions' said Lucy slowly.

'And?', replied Caroline Westbrooke in a coaxingly playful tone of voice, twisting her body about upon the sofa to look up at Lucy from all of three inches distant. 'Have you three good answers then my lady?! Or have', she concluded, after skipping to her feet and putting hands on hips, ' I outwitted you for once?!'

'You are more than capable of that when you set a mind to it. But not upon this occasion.'

'Then pray tell me your conclusions', Caroline responded with a pert smile as she sat down again.

'Mr Fuller supposed', began Lucy meeting the eyes of her now engrossed companion, 'that Isabella Arcachon was involved in the plot. In general, as we now know,from his remarks in part to you, but also to both Miss Stott and Anne Lunsford, he had a contempt for women. Also, since Isabella was recent married, such flattery could not avail him. So it was either a liaison between them or a comment upon her position in society and its connections and allegiance. I had, and have, no cause from Isabella to suspect the first. So it must surely have been the second.'

'Yes I see. But oh I am not yet started and you are done already. I should have called for Susan as you did for Henrietta', said Miss Westbrooke, referring to the fact that Lucy was dressed and ready while she was still sitting there with a dress on her lap and with hair to arrange. 'I will wear this pink and if you can attend to my coiffure- it will need little work anyway with most of my ringlets loose or near it- we can continue to talk undisturbed. I have the pins and ribbons here. Will you? And first help me with my gown?'

'Of course. Now as to Count Arcachon', said Mrs Ferrars as Miss Westbrooke stood now in her petticoats, 'my suspicions there was confirmed when his wife told me that he had spent four whole months in London straight after his marriage.'

'On pressing business I think', replied Caroline, wriggling into her fresh dress. Conversation then stalled until firstly all adjustments to that garment had been done and then, having sat down in front of her mirror, the necessary pins and ribbon had been given over for the second task.

'Yes', answered Lucy after the pause. 'Those words weighed much with me too. They was almost the outside of enough for a bridegroom with such a handsome bride. Most gentlemen would surely not behave so? Unless of course, such 'pressing business' was so important, secret, dangerous or perhaps all three, as to prevent anything delaying it? I thought straightway then that he was involved in the plotting. But upon which side? That I could not know and it took our little companion to find it out.'

'Yes indeed' said Caroline. handing over the fourth hairpin and closing the box lid upon the remainder. 'Meg was a dear creature and I do declare that had it not been for little Lydia I should have transported her back to live with us here in Queen Square! But what of Catherine Barbazon's words to Lucie Lavalle? We know that the Lavalles were opposed to Bonaparte and the poor duke's death was confirmation of that.'

Lucy nodded. 'That is puzzling true and I have two possible answers. One is that Mademoiselle Barbazon wished, as she had done before when contemplating you upon your gown, to divert the conversation. For in this instance Lucie Lavalle was accusing the Barbazons, quite correctly, of being Bonapartists. If you are being made muddy yourself the best, sometimes the only, way is to throw mud upon your opponent also. So that both might look the same. However there is another possibility. Which is that someone else - most likely Louisa Blandford as was - had given her to understand that the Lavalles were working against her and that she, Mademoiselle Barbazon, must cast doubts upon their loyalty. Whichever be the case the motive was little different. Is that all your thoughts now? Or are there more yet?'

'No that is all I think.'

'And does this work satisfy you', added Mrs Ferrars as, having tied the ribbon at the back of the profusion of tumbling curls, she now held up a small mirror.

'Indeed it does. You would have been a truly splendid lady's maid.'

'But for you my dear Caroline I might well have had to become one. For even had I been released I should not, with my background and reputation, have been easy welcomed back into society. Certainly that is what Miss Charlotte Cantlemere presumed. But she did not guess at your high regard for me and your great efforts because of it. If Mr Fuller was set upon your destruction she was as equal set upon mine. But now. Questions are answered. Gown is on. Hair is done. You have satisfaction?'

Caroline laughed and patted her on the shoulder 'Of course I have you clever thing! I stood before you in every way with ribbons not tied and but part dressed and you make all neat and ready for parading out - oh - two hundred years from now I dare say.'

Lucy matched laugh to laugh and just as easily. 'I had never imagined mysteries as states of undress! But I should have guessed that you would see it so! Bonnets shawls and all.'

A mischievously giggling Caroline began to sashay around the room. 'Well you can just stop your teasing of me Mrs Lucy Ferrars! Or perhaps, now your marriage is all done away with, you think that naughty Miss Lucy Steele may come alive again?! Well, whoever you think yourself to be, you will be interested in this. For it is a letter from Isabella. Which I shall not read however', concluded Miss Westbrooke posing, 'until you have given me an opinion upon this gown!'

'It is exceeding pretty Caroline and suits you very well. I do mean that. It really does.'

'Very well. Those praises will suffice! So I will now read it you.'

'My dear Miss Westbrooke.

I must tell you what has happened since your return to Bath. For it will both interest and amuse. All is something of the same song with the gentlemen of York. Mr John Saxby is typical in being quite forlorn without you. .And, though I do not frequent the place, I am

146

reliably informed by two of my own maids that those men also of such uncertain temper and base desires that drink at the 'Black Boy' are now so much your devotees that one word or suggestion that does not marry up the three words Miss Caroline Westbrooke with the three of beautiful sweet angel are set fair to cause a riot. You have, in short, and not at all to my surprise, enslaved the entire male population. One however I am resolved that you shall not retain is Mr Saxby. I am a free woman and shall break your spell upon him. Philippe being hanged and all Barbazons dead with him there is little else on that head. Mademoiselle Lucie Lavalle, a young lady much admiring of your friend Mrs Ferrars by the by, is to travel to London with her mother very soon. Where I understand she is to meet up once more with Miss Blandford. A curious girl that, though I do not dislike her. I shall end now as Mr Saxby is to pay a call this afternoon. He is most charming as always. Only with you did his tongue tie itself up in his boots. Well you have a sweet disposition and I cannot find it in my heart to resent it. Provided that is you keep your abundant charms well distant from his gaze until I have secured him. Fondest regards to yourself and Mrs Ferrars.

Your true friend.

Isabella. '

It was a pleasant letter after all the trials the two ladies had undergone and a relief to both to laugh over its contents. But one hour later the mood was very different as Caroline again began to read, this time to herself. For another piece of correspondence had been delivered. By special messenger for Miss Westbrooke from London and by order of Lord James Minto. Lucy had never taken her eyes from her friend's face and became increasingly concerned to see firstly the light hearted merriment vanish to seriousness and then that as rapidly be replaced with trembling lips and tears. Having finished her task Caroline got up and rushed to the window. Suddenly she turned around and, if a little more composed, was still in a state of high emotion. Lucy took her by the hand.

'Come. Sit down and tell me.'

'Oh Lucy .It is terrible. Lord Minto tells of a battle. Fought off Cape Trafalgar. He wanted us to be one of the very first to learn of it. We are owed that he says.'

'That is most thoughtful and raises him somewhat in my eyes. Though I have no doubt he considered you, and not myself, in that desire. What occurred then at this Cape Trafalgar?'

'It seems that Lord Nelson sighted the enemy fleet upon the twenty first. Battle was joined later that day and he gave the command 'England expects that every man will do his duty'.Then.. then.'

'Go on' said Lucy, taking Caroline's hands in hers.

'Well' continued Miss Westbrooke, drawing comfort from the gesture, 'Lord Nelson was standing on the quarterdeck of his ship. The 'Victory'. She had engaged several of the enemy vessels, one of which was the 'Redoutable'. It was then that..that..he was shot. Oh Lucy. He is dead. Lord Nelson is dead. I cannot believe it.'

In a day or so the whole country would now feel the grief which Caroline was expressing and none would do it with more genuine emotion.Yet such was the esteem in which this man was held that his passing would affect those usually far less prone to tenderness. It was a long long time since any tears had trickled their way down Mrs Lucy Ferrars' cheeks and, if she checked them after four, it was still a most significant quartet.

'And the battle?' she enquired of Caroline after a few moments. ' What of that?'

'A.... complete - triumph', Miss Westbrooke responded brokenly through the sobs.' We have lost no ships and they seventeen or eighteen.'

'Then England is saved. He has not died for naught. Yet we must pay an important call and take a long carriage drive to do it. For surely there will be one with more of a heavy heart than any other?'

Seated opposite to them at Merton, Lady Emma Hamilton smiled sadly at Caroline's offer to be the guest of herself and her father at Tinterton Manor.

'I thank you for that most kind thought Miss Westbrooke. Before he departed for Portsmouth on that fateful night Lord Nelson spoke of your good nature and that I might regard you as a true friend. It is evident that he was not mistaken. But no. England has no place for me. My reason for living has gone. We shall though, embrace as such friends and that is something I would not wish to do with most of my sex in society. Remember me as I was and look to yourself. You have much to live for. And much to give.'

Having warmly said her farewells to Caroline, Emma now turned to Lucy.

'Goodbye Mrs Ferrars. As one who has already climbed the hill to the top may I offer you some advice?'

'I should welcome it Lady Hamilton.'

'The day may come' said Emma giving her a keen look, 'when you, also, may wish to vanish. To become no more than a memory. As I soon shall be. A person in flesh and blood only to those who knew you. My world was destroyed by a frenchman's sharp sight and better aim, but there are other weapons. Take care they do not ruin what you have built.'

Lucy looked back at her. 'Lord Minto for one, considers me still something of a mystery I think your ladyship. If I see a danger of that being removed I shall do as you advise.'

Emma held the gaze.

'I hand you my torch Mrs Ferrars.The torch of one who has annoyed society by her great presumption to another who can do the same. Let it burn bright on top of your hill when you get there. As I am very sure you will. And, for my sake as well as your own, do not catch fire from it.'

With that thought, as Lady Emma Hamilton's guests made their departure, the most famous, or, to some, most infamous, woman of her day passed into the pages of both fact and fiction. Her adventures were now over. Unlike those of Miss Caroline Westbrooke and Mrs Lucy Ferrars. Or was it now Miss Lucy Steele reborn?

But that is another story.

THE END

7055149R00088

Printed in Great Britain
by Amazon.co.uk, Ltd.,
Marston Gate.